Rider of the Crimson Dragon

Master story teller

I just finished reading the Kindle version of The Adventures of Luzi Cane, Book 2. The author is indeed a master story teller! While including delightful experiences and awareness of elves and dragons, she weaves in incredible wisdom, clarity, and light about our journey to remember who we are and why we're here.

I absolutely love the development of the characters in the story. Luzi and her daughter Julia (even before her birth) are so real and vibrant and full of wonderful wisdom and love!

I am an avid reader, and when I wake up the day after finishing a book, wondering what the characters are up to today, I know the book is an extraordinary creation!

If you ever find yourself wondering about the "big" questions about how to realize who you are and how to experience your life to the fullest, I heartedly recommend reading The Adventures of Luzi Cane!

- Patricia M. Severance

The Adventures of Luzi Cane

Rider of the Crimson Dragon

by Eriqa Queen

Series title: The Adventures of Luzi Cane
Title: Rider of the Crimson Dragon
Copyright © Eriqa Queen 2019
Copyright © Erik Istrup Publishing 2019
Cover art by Ricardo Robles Copyright © 2019
Published through Ingram Spark
Font: Palatino
ISBN: 978-87-92980-35-9

Genre: Fantasy

Other titles in the series:
The Soul of the White Dragon (Book 1)
Return of the Unicorn (Book 3)
The Truth of the Black Dragon (Book 4)
A total of six titles are planned

Erik Istrup Publishing
Jyllandsgade 16 stth, 9610 Nørager, Danmark
www.erikistrup.dk/publishing/
eip@erikistrup.dk

Contents

Another time, another place 7

Lucia Cane 17

Meeting the Merlin 21

My birthday 31

Ythr penn Dragwn 41

Apostles 45

Merlin 48

Having kids 52

Meeting in Elvendale 57

What happened in MY past lives? 62

Past and future lives 63

What IS past and future? 69

The Crimson Dragon 71

Presenting Shaumbra 74

Anasazi 79

Meeting our daughter-to-be 81

Ancient America 87

The earliest writing 97

Noah's Ark 98

Moses and Abraham 107

Some early scripts 113

A Chinese wedding 121

Ju-long, about his dad 152

Ting and Cheng.. 156

Ju-long's father 161

Meeting Kong again 178

The bracelet.. 187

Kong's dream 194

The fishing trip 216

Kong's future... 232

Nikola Tesla.. 241

Brain versus consciousness.............................. 246

A free mind 248

Personal energy 249

From energy to solid matter 250

AI vs. limitless energy 252

Energy and life 258

Time is energy 261

What's to come 263

Allowing, Un- & AND 267

The birth of Julia... 274

Author's Comments... 277

Additional stuff 279

Sources.. 281

Another time, another place

I'm sitting in a horse-driven carriage rumbling through the cold night of early winter. It has not started to snow, but it is raining and a storm is coming up. I am wearing a heavy and thick, long dress in red-brown colours and long, dark-brown boots with laces. I'm in the rear seat and my two children are sitting in the other seat, facing me. The boy is ten and the girl eight. We are all scared, fighting desperately to hold on to something to prevent being thrown around in the small compartment.

The horses are snorting and the crack of the driver's whip is cutting through the rain that is drumming on the roof. I fear the carriage will soon fall apart.

We have reached the forest now. I can hear it because the softer ground has reduced the noise from the wheels and the hooves. Shortly after, the carriage stops and the driver's voice reaches us through the door.

"We'll just check the carriage, harness and the horses. Then we'll continue. Please stay inside."

I pull away the curtain, but I cannot see anything because of the rain on the glass, so I open the window a bit. The cold wind and the rain are blowing on my face. The horses are black and I can only see them because their wet bodies reflect the moonlight. I wish for more clouds to cover the Moon and more rain to cover our tracks. The men are talking behind the horses and now a faint light reaches me.

Shortly after, they walk around the carriage and then climb back up. A cry from the driver, a crack of his whip, and we are back on the run to safety. I close and secure the window and draw the curtain. The road is still bumpy, but now it is more roots than rocks that are in the way.

The sway of the carriage must finally have made me doze off, because I wake up now that it suddenly stops. The driver opens the door.

"You'll stay here for the night, getting some food and a place to sleep. We'll drive on to lead pursuers off the track."

I see that the man is exhausted.

"You and your assistant have been up all day and half of the night, working hard. I demand that you get a good meal and a few hours of sleep, otherwise you won't get far. Make sure that the horses are tended to."

"Yes, ma'am, but please go inside."

The children are woken and we step outside. Everything is wet and there is a strong smell of wet dirt and plants. The driver and his assistant carry the children up to a log house on two levels. The door is open and a man and two women are waiting for us.

The driver, François, gives orders to free the horses from the carriage and lead them to a shack to be dried with hay, fed and watered.

I turn to the driver. "Have you brought saddles in case you have to leave the carriage?"

"Yes, ma'am, we have two on top." He points up at the top of the carriage.

The man in the doorway introduces himself and the two ladies as Monsieur Rémy Paquit, his wife, Femma, and her sister, Celine. The women run back to the fireplace to get some food ready. Shortly after, we are presented with hot soup, bread, cheese and a little piece of smoked sheep's meat.

I look at the people around me. The children wear fine clothes, which do not match the primitive accommodation. The driver and his assistant are still wet, even though they wore oilskin covers during the trip. The man wears trousers and a white shirt, over which he has an apron. The two women wear common dresses and have scarves covering their hair. I see no kids.

The ground floor is mostly one large room, with a fireplace and cooking facilities at one end. There is a door near the fireplace, probably leading to some sleeping quarters, which benefit from the heat from the fireplace. The large room contains a long table in the middle and a few smaller ones near the walls, all with simple chairs. There are guest rooms on the first floor.

My children have finished the meal and cannot keep their eyes open, so they are carried upstairs and put to bed. There is a place ready for me as well. I kiss them goodnight and plan on sitting there while they fall asleep, but they doze off immediately. After a quick pee in the pot by the bed, I decide to go to bed as well, too tired to go downstairs to thank our hosts.

I wake up with a cry, terrified and confused. I find my boyfriend, Ju-long, peacefully sleeping beside me. My digital alarm clock shows 3:33 in blue light.

"What a dream!"

Not quite awake yet, I walk to the bathroom, lucky that the floor is heated. The light hurts my eyes and I must close them and then slowly open them again while sitting on the toilet.

"It was so real, as if I had been there!"

I feel a presence of another being in my heart, and a greeting comes through. It is a friend.

"I AM the Ascended Master Saint Germain, of the Beloved Saint Germain."

"Greetings, Saint Germain. This time we do not meet in the shower!"

"These days you're usually not alone in the shower and I wouldn't take your focus off Ju-long, even if it would be possible."

"But you wouldn't mind changing my focus while I'm peeing."

"You're not peeing, it's just your body. You are consciousness, not your body, you know. Your focus IS on the dream, or what you think is a dream."

"It surely feels real; the fear, all the senses, even the rain on my face! I can still feel it."

"What you experienced was that you relived a short glimpse from another life."

"And why would I do that?"

"First, you don't have to be so upset. You're totally safe. This memory is probably triggered by some immediate possibilities in your life."

"When did it happen?"

"It happened in the beginning of June 1793 in France, just after the French Revolution, during the Reign of Terror, where the revolution backfired. Your family was not against the revolution per se, but you strongly opposed the terror, violence and inhumane behaviour against the overthrown families and anyone else that may not have been in favour, which was the Reign of Terror."

"Please, tell me more about this!"

"Oh no, I think you must go to bed now. You can look all this up on your computer tomorrow."

A faint kiss lands on my forehead, a gentle touch in my heart and I am alone again. I feel tired, finish up and walk back to bed. Ju-long hasn't moved and I curl up under his sheet, feeling his warm body on my cold skin. He moves a little and puts an arm around me. I feel safe and drift off into sleep.

Now I am back in the log house in the forest, sitting at the large table and eating breakfast, consisting of porridge and a mug of warm beer. I can hear the children playing outside. They are laughing, which soothes me. The man of the house, Monsieur Paquit, comes through the front door and takes a seat at the opposite side of the table, looking me straight in the eyes.

"You and the kids have to be going when you've finished. We have prepared two horses that your driver left before they took off earlier. He has paid for the two saddles and the gear. My wife will prepare some food for you to take along, and one of my trusted men will escort you to your next stop. Then he will return by a different route."

I nod, but am terrified. The man goes outside again and his wife's sister, Celine, serves me a mug of tea. While drinking the tea with both hands around the mug, I think back on the events that took place just before we left our home.

It is early morning. A servant of the house comes to me in a great hurry, telling me that a messenger has arrived and that it is urgent for him to see me. He has a message from my husband. I run outside, where the horseman is still catching his breath while drinking water brought by one of the stable-boys who happened to be passing by with a bucket of water with a ladle for the workers in the stables.

"I have a verbal message from your husband,

ma'am. You and your children must leave immediately without wasting your time on packing. The uprising has gone out of control and you're no longer safe. I have some directions for your driver."

"What about my husband? Is he all right?"

"For the moment, yes, but he can't risk coming here to be with you at this moment. Get ready and get me the driver."

The driver is fetched by the stable-boy and, while I prepare the children, the driver gets his instructions. I come out with the children, who are quite confused about all this commotion, and I see that six horses are being pulled to the carriage. We usually use just four. All the people around me show grave or anxious faces. The messenger is talking with the driver, François, and René, whom he must have selected as his assistant. They are both armed with guns. It does not seem much use to me, since it probably would be sheer luck if they hit anything while sitting on the carriage at full speed on a bumpy road. Severin from the kitchen and some of the girls bring two baskets, one for us in the carriage and one for the men on the driver's seat. Bottlenecks are showing above the rims of the baskets. Probably wine and water. Boys from the stables show up with rain shawls for the drivers, and two girls come running with blankets, that are placed inside the carriage. I drive the kids inside and ask them to be quiet. The door slams behind us, and I haven't sat down before I fall onto the seat as the carriage jumps forward.

"The horses are ready and some provisions have been packed as well. There are some rain shawls, but they are quite large for the kids. I have planned for the girl to sit in front of you, and the boy will have the other horse. Please get your things, ma'am."

The weather is dry for the moment, but I see dark clouds in the direction from where the wind is coming. I explain to the children that we must move on right away, and the girl starts to cry. The boy is lifted to his horse by Monsieur Paquit and, when I am seated, he lifts the girl and places her in front of me. She eventually calms down and we follow Monsieur Paquit's servant, who rides a dark-brown horse. I have confidence in his riding skills. The boy rides in the middle.

A hand is gently stroking my face, and Ju-long's gentle voice reaches me over the centuries.

"Luzi, it's all right. You're shaking; it's just a dream."

I open my eyes. I am sweating, but feel the cold follow me out of the dream.

"Yes, I know it's a dream and, when I've written it down, I'll tell you about it. Could you please make us some peppermint tea while I'm writing this in my notebook? I feel it's just what I need."

"As you wish, ma'am!"

He smiles, happy that I seem to be all right. I follow his naked body, covered by only his tight underwear, before he walks into the kitchen.

He returns with a salver when I am about halfway through my typing, climbs into bed and sits patiently, waiting for me to finish the story. When I am finished, he places the salver on our legs and I start on my story.

"This night, I have this very real dream, and Saint German visited me and gave me the hint that it could be a memory from another life, probably triggered by some immediate possibilities in my life."

After I have finished, Ju-long is silent for a bit and I can see that he does not quite know what to say.

"I really hope that you'll not be chased by an angry mob on your way to work!"

"Don't be silly. It could be something about the feelings I had during the dream, but Saint Germain said that I am completely safe."

"Well, I'm glad to hear that. You seem to be OK again, right?"

"Yes, I'm fine. I'm just wondering: if it's happening in France, why, then, do I speak English in the dream?"

Later, while I'm getting dressed, I realize that the house we are living in now is older than the events

happening in my dream, maybe as much as two
hundred years, which is as much as eight generations.

Lucia Cane

I was born in Hong Kong in 1989, grew up there and went to an English school in my earlier years. My father is English and my mother is Chinese. My father was, and still is, a businessman, and my mother, who earlier attended my dad's business, is now spending her time with the things she loves: decorating, painting and gardening.

My sister, Anna, is six years younger than me. We moved to London when I was 18. Being half Caucasian, half Asian, I inherited a long, slender body from my father and the Asian looks, including my black hair, from my mother. With Anna, it is more the other way around, and she has brown hair. I still have my grandparents on my mother's side, living in Hong Kong.

I study history, prehistory, ancient cultures in general, ethnographical studies, literature and journalism. As a source of income, I work as a freelance writer. In addition to that, I work as a copywriter, and as editor of books for some universities, collecting data for colleges and helping them to edit the materials. I also do some book-writing, and it is more book-writing than book-selling, but there is nothing new in that.

As a tool in my work I use a smartphone but, while working, I turn off all private messages since they are a huge distraction and greatly reduce my productivity and efficiency. I do not want to be a slave of technology, it must work FOR me. You may shake your head when I tell you that I use a paper notebook as well. I use the camera in my phone quite often, a lot of the time to pick up text from various sources. I may use the voice recorder on the phone as well. When I write large volumes of text, I need to use a real keyboard, since I use all ten fingers; otherwise, production would be too low.

Ju-long is my boyfriend and from a Chinese family. We went to school together in Hong Kong, but got separated when I moved to London. During some research for a book about Elves and Little People in an ethnographic perspective, I followed some Chinese clues and ended up at the library in Hong Kong where Ju-long was working at the time. We reconnected, and are now living in Brighton on the south coast of England. Ju-long is at Brighton University, with campuses in Eastbourne and Hastings, studying, teaching, and doing some work in the British Library in London, because of its huge collection of Chinese material. Ju-long has his mother and her parents in Hong Kong.

My connections are to the University of London and the University of Kent, Tonbridge Centre; the latter is situated midway between London and Brighton, and can be reached in a little more than an hour by train. For now, we live in a hired house of stone, dating from the 1600s.

I feel that I must give you a little more background if you haven't followed me from my first adventure. Last year I was once again watching the movie *The Lord of the Rings* with my friend, Cassandra. Shortly afterwards, I entered the Elven world in a dream, where I met the woman, Josela. She told me that they call themselves Sidhe, like they do in Ireland. The name is pronounced "she". Josela showed me that I visit Elvendale in an altered state of consciousness and that it is as real as what I consider the real, physical world. She also told me about reincarnation, but I will not go into details about this subject here.

Later, I met the white Birman cat, Loong, in Shanghai, China. The name means "dragon". It turns out that Loong is a dragon soul and connects to Elvendale. As he says, "I'm not a dragon, but consciousness just like yourself. I just choose to appear as a cat in the human world to get a better connection with the physical. The dragon that I normally choose to appear as in Elvendale is partly because I connect to China now, which has a long tradition of dragon worship, partly because I work with the same virtues as the knights and because I'm simply fascinated by this creation. It's not, of course, to be worshipped, but because the consciousness has that focus."

Josela told me that the Sidhe eventually must have experiences on the physical Earth, so they will really benefit from a softening of the human life. The life of the Sidhe is not as physical as ours, so incarnating in the human world, into a human life, will be quite harsh.

Now I often connect with Elvendale to meet Josela, Loong and other friends. What I really like about

Elvendale is that, here, it's much lighter and more joyful than the human world. Here I learned about my true purpose in this lifetime, which gave me a much clearer understanding of my life up till now and the path that I choose in my human life. As I get more experienced in being aware that I am consciousness embodied in human form with a mind, it is easier to do my real work. The true way to change the world is to connect to human consciousness, as all human beings are. By being aware of what I sense will benefit humanity, I can inject this into human consciousness. When some people are ready to take up that task, they can tap into this knowledge. Often this knowledge is based on my discussions with the Sidhe and others of high consciousness. You may compare it with being a member of, for example, Greenpeace, without needing the direct confrontation, which always produces a reactive force. I work without force.

Part of humanity will always live to experience 'the darkness', like power in any form, abuse in both ways, self-destruction, hunger and so on. Another part is truly looking for a lighter way to experience life and, although there are lots of distractions along the way, they may eventually tap into the knowledge to a better way. One could say that your 'energy' will always guide you in the 'right' direction. Heavy energy will guide you to the 'dark' experiences, while a lighter energy gives you other opportunities. There is no judgement to any of this - it is just the way things work. We must all live both extremes to get the full experience of life.

Meeting the Merlin

At the university, I have just started a new project with two students. It is about gathering historical facts and distinguishing them from other, less legitimate, sources. Those who write history are usually the winning parties, and such history is always coloured by their interpretations, how they justify their actions and put themselves in a most glorious light and, at the same time, point fingers at their opponents.

Christopher, or Chris for short, and Steven, or Steve for short, are some joyful guys, but serious when it comes to their studies. Otherwise, I would not have taken on being their mentor and co-writer. By choosing to be part of the project, I can refer to it as partly my work, and the guys will benefit from my experience in writing and going into great depth in my search for data as well as my many sources.

The benefit of me being five or six years older than them is that I can act with more authority, and thus use less energy on pushing them forward all the time. They have quickly learned what I expect from them and they see an honour in doing their best to keep me in a good mood. It may sound as if I keep cracking the whip over their heads, but we level out of mutual respect when we are together.

The working title of our project is, for now, *The Truth Behind the Written History and How to Obtain*

It. A little too long and too broad, but it guides us for now. We have not yet decided what era or subject we will cover. First, we must find out where the most data lies, and then we can narrow our focus or perspective.

It is said that history is written by the victorious, but finding data from the conquered may prove likewise to be unreliable for the same reasons; the objective would be to put the victorious in a bad light.

It has proven quite difficult to retrieve data with a high degree of reliability, and definitely not in an amount that in any way gives enough content to our project. In his despair, Chris claims that it would be easier to build a time machine and travel back in time to record the actual events.

After some reluctance on my part, I tell Chris and Steve about my dreams, what apparently should have happened during the French Revolution.

Steve's reaction comes promptly.

"It can't, in any way, be used as proof of ANYTHING, and it's really just a dream, even it felt quite real."

He is right, of course. Nothing that comes from what appears to be a dream will be taken seriously. Still, I urge them to write down anything they encounter in dreams, so-called daydreams, or events that they find unusual.

If I am to get anywhere with these guys, I must get them into the idea of mass consciousness, and how everyone is connected to this common field of memories. I know that we won't be able to prove the truth of the material we present from this method, but we may be able to get the authenticity and, thereby, select the right leads to follow in historical data.

It is the evening on the day prior to my birthday. I lie on the sofa, not far from the lit fireplace, waiting for Ju-long to get home. I smile to myself; he must be out shopping for 'the exact right thing' for my birthday present. I feel my love for him in my heart. I don't care about the present; I just want him to get home so I can snuggle up in his arms, sensing him in every way, enjoying his smell, feeling his touch and kisses. My heart is wide open as my love for him pours out.

After a while, as I start to doze off, a gentle greeting reaches me and I feel the presence of the assented master, Count Saint Germain.

"Greetings, dear. You are particularly happy this day."

"When connecting to Ju-long, I always am. The strange thing is that I'm not waiting for him, in the usual meaning of the word 'wait'. I enjoy these moments where we connect heart to heart, as they are at least as real as holding him."

"Indeed. In the physical meeting, you mostly use your basic human senses because they are more predominant."

"I know I'm always posing you a lot of questions when we meet, but I really have a challenge getting my project with Steve and Chris on the road. I have got this idea that we could go back in time to pick up what really happened in history."

"You can't go back to the absolute truth, since every potential, which means the ones not 'lived out', is as real as the ones that were actually played out. You COULD find the one that most probably took place in your 3D reality."

"How can potentials be as real as the ones lived out, and where do these potentials come from?"

"All these potentials burst into existence when THE ONE CONSCIOUSNESS or, as I call it, The Eternal One, abbreviated to Theo, desired to experience itself. All the potentials that it saw possible came to be, as consciousness, which you call the soul, bursts out in the image of Theo as well as energy to be the material to create from, solid or not solid. You may see the potentials as blueprints for different clay pots, the clay being energy and the soul being the potter. Since space-time does not really exist, all pots are already made, and now the potter is experiencing how the pots were made. The space-time is a tool for experiencing the potentials."

"What about my own experiences? They must be more real than the potentials."

"As all pots are made, none of them is less real. All your lives do not happen one after the other, so there is no past or future in that and, at the same time, all the potentials are happening at the same 'time' as well. It is only from a human standpoint that it is perceived to be linear and that is as it should be. Even the 'now' is an illusion, because the 'now' will always be the past. So, every event is happening now and the space-time is passing through the events to add the illusion of past and future. You'll never find the absolute truth or, more correctly, every event is true."

"Then it would make no sense to continue?!"

"I would not say that. You could put together a series of events that you sense are happening in a series in 3D, influenced by space-time and consciousness."

"But then it will be just a good story and not historical fact!"

"It will be a true story!"

"If I take my calendar and trace back every event recorded, then it is a true line of events."

"Yes, but it's only ONE line of events from all possible lines of events, and only experienced from one narrow perspective, from one camera angle if you wish. I suggest you use your method of connecting events as much as you can, to make your intellect or mind at peace. At the same time, I want you to remember how frustrated you are right now, when you have to convince your fellow-students to follow your thoughts about past lives and past events."

"You're so right. To Steve and Chris, it's difficult, or even impossible, to grasp this view."

"The best way to keep your sanity is to see one line of events, where each event is realized into this particular line out of the many different potentials."

"I imagine that mass consciousness is part of this reality, so we could dive into it to retrieve data."

"Mass consciousness of this Earth is created by this reality, BUT it is built of ANY human thoughts, feelings, perceptions and belief. You'll even meet Santa Claus here, so you must recognize him as real too, which he is, since he was created by man and to some extent based on a real person."

"I can see that mass consciousness is a hot, swirling soup one could dive really deep into and get completely lost."

The sound of the latch of the outbuilding door reaches me, and I open my eyes. Ju-long is hiding his present for me there, so I must remember not to go into the outbuilding today. Saint Germain makes a low bow, gives us his blessings and pulls away.

I close my eyes, pretending to sleep as Ju-long comes into the living room. I open my eyes.

"Oh, you're back!"

26

Ju-long has a tall, slender body, Asian features, short, slightly messed, black hair and brown eyes. He wears tight blue jeans and a tight red T-shirt with an embroidered dragon in warm colours on the chest. He is barefoot. He is warm after his journey.

I stretch my arms towards him, urging him to come to me on the sofa, well knowing that he would have done so anyway.

"Hi, love. Nice to find you lying here on the sofa and with the fireplace lit."

"I wasn't intending anything but, since you're here, I might as well take advantage of it."

Later we make dinner in a joint venture, as we usually do in my family, and eat it sitting on some pillows near the fireplace, watching a movie. The warmth and the wine make me sleepy and, before the movie has finished, Ju-long carries me to bed.

I wake up at 3:03 am. An event from the night that stands out is where I meet two young men, whom I recognize as Chris and Steve, though they did not look like them.

I am in nature and the night sky is filled with stars. The air is so clear that the Milky Way shines its white, curving body over the whole sky, like a grandiose river. I am a male, a teacher of some kind, and my two students, for the time being, are sitting close to the fire preparing a meal. It looks like soup of some kind. They are cold and have the hoods on their cowls pulled over their heads. They are chatting in low voices, so as not to disturb me. We have camped not far from the road, and now I see a figure coming towards us, following a narrow path of dry dirt made from the many feet of the people who have previously used this place. A man's voice reaches us as the person in a cowl greets us.

"Greetings; I am Lord Hameth the Merlin."

My two students get quickly on their feet, bow and then stand, looking down. Lord Hameth pulls the hood away from his head and shows us a timeless face, kind and wise.

"I'm known as a great storyteller because of my many journeys, not only in this time, but through time and beyond time. Will you share your fire with me in return for some good stories?"

I feel confused, since I sense that this is Saint Germain who is visiting us. He must have his reasons to appear as Merlin. With one hand, I show him to a tree stump not too close to the fire, which I earlier had selected to be my seat at the fire.

"Yes, of course. Please take a seat, Lord Hameth."

I can see that the young man I now know as Steve is bursting to ask a question.

"So, you're really Merlin!?"

"I am a Merlin, because Merlin is a title. You could say 'The Merlin', because there is only one Merlin at a time."

Chris has now found the courage to ask a question too.

"Doesn't Merlin wear a pointed hat?"

"Oh, no. The pointed hat, as you know it, is much later in history than the time we're in now, around five hundred years after Christ. The pointed hat derived from very old times, where some used a cone-shaped hat of metal to amplify the brainwaves."

Chris asks the next, obvious, question.

"So, it's the time of King Arthur?!"

"I'm called upon by Ythr penn Dragwn, the father of Arthur to be, as well as the Apostles, so I've taken physical form to be of service at these troublesome times."

"So, you are helping us to beat the Saxons?"

"No, I'm here to unify a region and to prevent Christianity from getting away from its original core. It's only a few centuries ago that Christianity took physical form and, already, the Bible has been ripped of many of the essential truths. The church is fighting the real magic and what they call the false religions. Did you know that pagan means 'simple spirit'? The spirits of Earth take many faces, faces that people can relate to. Yes, most people in these times may have an ordinary approach to this, but they feel the connection nevertheless."

Now I too feel the need to ask a question.

"What have Uther and the Apostles in common? I really don't see the connection."

"They don't have much in common, other than the common oppressor. King Uther sees that the Christian church is trying to wipe out the pagan connection to nature and the nature spirits, cutting off the grounding of the body and mind from the Earth, from which both mind and body derive. The Apostles, meaning messengers, see that the true messages are being distorted and amputated by the same church. The church even pulls in pagan deities to lure people into the Christian faith."

Chris leans forward, with gleaming eyes.

"Please, tell us about King Arthur and Camelot!"

"Oh, I think you have got enough to ponder for a while; but we may meet again, so there will be time for other stories. I bid you farewell. I am The Merlin."

Lord Hameth gets up, bows and walks back the way he had come. It seems to me that he slowly dissolves into complete transparency before he reaches the road.

After having gone through this event in my mind, I pick my pen and notebook from the drawer in the bedside table and write down the episode. Now I am so sleepy than I haven't the strength to put the notebook and pen back in the drawer, and doze off.

My birthday

I wake up to a nice smell of breakfast; toast and coffee. I remember that it is my 27th birthday and open my eyes. Ju-long has just come through the bedroom door with a salver loaded with all kinds of nice things, including a slender, crystal vase with a red rose, which I'm sure he has picked in the garden. Ju-long smiles widely. He has been busy in the kitchen and is sweating. He looks gorgeous. As I take the napkin, a small present is revealed underneath.

"Happy birthday, love!"

I can imagine that he has taken quite some time to pick the 'right' thing for me. I wait until he is back in bed before I start to open the small gift. It's a little heavy for so small a thing. I get rid of the paper and sit with a small, light-blue cardboard box. Slowly I open it.

"Wow!"

It takes a little time to examine the thing.

Ju-long comments:

"It's made of bronze. You have many chains, most likely one in gold will go with it. It's called a harmony bell."

It is a bronze pendant; two hollow, semi-ball shells kept together with a small hinge and a lock. One shows a tree-trunk with branches and roots, creating a web. The other one is made of eight outlines of hearts, which create a web as well. It looks like a small cage and is about one inch in diameter. Inside the cage is a blue ball, which can be seen through the web on both sides. It makes a sound when I rattle it.

"Thank you, love. It is lovely and very special. I'll wear it today."

I kiss him, careful not to spill anything that is on the salver.

We are both out of the house today. Ju-long is going to the university here in Brighton and I am heading to London.

On my way to London University, I doze off on the train with the intention of asking Saint Germain about the dream with Merlin and the two students.

Sure enough, I find myself in an old study together with Saint Germain. We are sitting in two comfortable armchairs with a small coffee table between us. The table holds an elegant salver with beautiful china, two cups with silver spoons and a small bowl of sugar lumps. There is a smell of jasmine tea in the room.

"Hello, Luzi, welcome to my study."

"Hello and thank you, Saint Germain. Where are we?"

"We're in my study in Louisenlund Manor in Güby, close to Eckernförde, Germany, where I lived as Count St Germain until 1784."

"It's in an old style, but looks quite new."

"Yes, it's only about five years old. The manor was built between 1772 and 1776 for Prince Charles of Hesse-Kassel as a gift for his wife, Princess Louise of Denmark. I have a study and a laboratory here provided by the prince."

"Oh, I see. That's interesting."

"Would you care for some tea?"

Saint Germain points to the teapot.

"Yes, please."

Saint Germain pours tea for both of us. I reach over and use the sugar tongs to drop one lump of sugar in my cup. The cup is made of very fine and delicate china. Saint Germain answers before I can formulate the simple question in my mind.

"Yes, it's genuine Chinese china."

I pick up the cup and stir, but the tea is still too hot to drink so I smell it instead. I get to my question.

"I wanted to meet you to know what the dream

with the Merlin was really about."

"It was not a dream of the mind, but an event we created - a dimension, you might say - to trigger your young students' imaginative creative abilities. You'll meet them today, and they may agree that dreams can be more than just the mind rearranging information. Dreams can be real."

"So Merlins go way back in history?"

"The first Merlin took physical form at the same time as we started to impose the Christ consciousness onto human consciousness around 630 years before Yeshua was born."

"Who can be a Merlin?"

"The Merlin was an accented master, but there have not been any embodied Merlins in the last 400 years, counting your present time."

"What was the occupation of the Merlins?"

"The Merlins worked closely with the Mystery Schools to bring more understanding and clarity to humanity. It is done most efficiently if you are an embodied master. You need the body to firmly connect to humanity and mass consciousness."

"So Yeshua and the Merlins were doing the same thing, bringing illumination to humanity."

"And so are you! Don't forget that!"

"I tend to forget it in my daily work, but I feel it

most of the time."

"That's all right. It's just the mind that forgets it, and that's good, since the mind can't do it anyway. It is the feeling, the sensing of your SELF, the light of the soul, you, the consciousness, that is at work."

"I've had a thought about the cone-shaped metal hat that you talked about last night as the Merlin. That is the technique that is used today in the EMP engine, EMP meaning Electromagnetic Pulse. Microwaves are amplified in the cone-shaped engine part to get a boost that can propel the engine forward. The engine does not need any fuel, and uses only energy for the control systems, including the energy to make the microwaves."

"The brain booster had very little effect. It was ancient knowledge that had been picked up but, without the true understanding of the function as well as the function of the brain, it was of little use. It is like trying to use magic without knowing the true magic. People would call true magic, 'The way God creates'."

"I assume that the true magic is the imaginative creation of the consciousness, right?"

"Indeed. Among other things, magic means 'multiple'; many, many appearances at the same time."

"Multiple, because the result of consciousness creation may come into the world in many forms."

I finish up my tea and feel it is time to leave Saint Germain.

"I always enjoy our talks. Now I'll meet with the two young men at London University in 2018!"

Saint Germain gets up and gives me his hand to say farewell.

I have found Dion Fortune's (1890-1946) definition of magic: "Magic is the art and science of causing change in consciousness in accordance with will."

Since true magic works directly with consciousness, the outcome may or may not have an effect in the physical world and, if it has, there is still the time factor that is in play.

Old Germanic users of rune magic believed that both the caster and the receiver must benefit from the action before it will take effect. I must assume that it is both humans that would have to benefit from the spell, but that is a human rule and consciousness is not biased to what is right or wrong, so the outcome might not be pleasant for the human part.

Another way of working with consciousness is found in the non-censured ancient Aramaic text, according to Neil Douglas Klotz: John 16, 23-24: *"Ask without hidden motive and be surrounded by your answer. Be enveloped by what you desire, that your gladness be full."* When you 'know' that you have already 'received' the answer, or 'thing', it will be there.

Chris is in our meeting room, reserved by me for two hours for a follow-up on our project about what really happened in the past. He greets me when I step in.

"Hi, Luzi. You look radiant today. I trust you had a good night's sleep?"

"Oh, it's my birthday and I was served breakfast in bed. I even got a nap on the train."

"Then happy birthday, dear Luzi. I dreamed about you last night."

"Oh. Do you remember anything of what happened in your dream?"

"Well. First, it was a very clear dream, or should I say real? Steve was there, too, and we were visited by Merlin!"

"Cool, Chris. What else can you tell?"

"As I said, the dream was very real. The only strange thing was that your face changed back and forth between yours and a man's, but he was not Chinese."

Now Steve comes into the room, after knocking.

"Hello! You both look quite excited. Is it something that you want to share?"

Chris starts off.

"First of all, it's Luzi's birthday!"

Steve shakes my hand.

"Happy birthday, my beautiful teacher! How old might you be?"

"Nice and rude at the same time. I have just turned 27, if it's so important for you to know."

Steve tries to soften me up.

"You don't look a day over twenty! And, by the way, I dreamed about you last night."

Chris looks surprised.

"You too?"

"And Merlin was giving us a lecture. Something about the Roman Catholic Church. You, Chris, asked him about the silly pointed hat. When you have the chance, you should ask for something more profound!"

I explain.

"Asking about the hat is just because Chris is obser-vant of the details."

Steve wants to move on with the reason why we are meeting.

"Let's stop this silly talk, and start on the project. We need to get it on the right track, if it's even mov-ing!"

Here I must be clear about the project to help them in not losing faith.

"I think it's moving but, before we continue, I have something to share with both of you."

Chris encourages me to proceed.

"Please share away, Luzi!"

"You've both dreamed about the three of us and Merlin, and I have too! Now, I want you to share as much as you can remember and, after that, I'll add my own experience."

Chris had picked up the most visual details of the two, while Steve had more of an insight of the persons he was together with, but he had a stereotypical image of Merlin with a pointed hat. He had picked up that Merlin had made many journeys, which Steve called time-travel. Chris had picked up that there have been many Merlins which, to him, was translated into that Merlin has had many lives. Now I add my version, as I was urged by Saint Germain to tell, that he was that particular incarnation of Merlin, by the name of Lord Hameth. He did this to prevent Chris and Steve focusing on the public understanding of Merlin, which would limit their understanding of the whole experience. Merlin was just the messenger and the figure to get their attention.

The room we are sitting in is quite small, and I have placed myself strategically at the small table with my back to the window. Then the young men will get the most sunlight and therefore energy into their systems, since the subject that is now starting to roll like a snowball down a hill, getting bigger and bigger while gaining weight and momentum, will demand as much energy from their systems as they can manage.

"So, boys, you must agree with me that this is no ordinary dream, or dreams. Saint Germain has called us into that experience, and remember that it's your consciousness that visits this event, not your mind and body. Your mind IS, however, aware of the event, or we could not express any of this in words. This should also prove to you that dreams can be from the mind, OR created by our consciousness to be a real place, not necessarily a physical place."

After this, we make a summary, which turns out to be like this:

One: Ythr penn Dragwn, I keep the spelling as I received it, was a pagan king who opposed the 'new' Christian faith, partly because it discarded the old belief of nature, and partly because 'new' normally equals 'bad'.

Two: The Apostles opposed the manipulative side of the church in its quest for power and wealth, since wealth could access even more power.

Three: Merlin is a title and time-travel IS possible, but not in the way that it is normally thought of.

This gives us three key points, one for each of us, and I ask Chris and Steve to close their eyes and feel into which one they consider themselves most attuned to, and then stick to that feeling without starting to mentalize pros and cons. Steve picks the Apostles, Chris takes Merlin, so Ythr penn Dragwn goes to the woman with her back to the window. Before we continue the meeting, I have a few last things for the boys.

"You must remember to sense into the information you find and you MUST take notes of your own feelings and thoughts during your research, since it may be hints or information that are in the energy of the subject, even if not presented in the research material. It should not be necessary to point out that you must pay special attention to what your dreams may bring you, both when you are asleep and when you are awake. Dreams are now a valid tool in our quest for the truth of history."

I do not tell them that there is no absolute truth, other than all experiences lived out, or that potentials are true and that the lies are hiding in mass consciousness. This must be for another time, if it needs to be.

Below is the information we gathered for the three subjects, and that we shared some days later.

Ythr penn Dragwn

Here is my contribution, starting out with Saint Germain explaining the name of the king.

"Ythr penn Dragwn. The name has several meanings. There is the obvious dragon pen. The pen, or enclosure, is the World, with two dragons, being the white crystal consciousness dragon and the red dragon of the Earth. They are not fighting or in opposition to each other. Another meaning is 'son of the dragon' or 'son of the dragons'. Today you would say 'Dragonson' as a surname. It could be read as 'father of the dragon(s)' as well. You see, there is no right interpretation. They are all valid."

"Should a dragon, representing the soil, not be black or brown?"

"The red colour lies deep in humanity as the symbol of the living being, Gaia, from the red, volcanic soil of the initial Lemuria, as well as the red and yellow ochre found in various places and the red fluid in the body without which it will die. You meet the black and the white colours in the yin-yang symbol. Here you clearly see the two dragons with their pointy tails. The dots are their souls, not their eyes. The Chinese name does not speak of a specific colour, but calls the symbol 'dark-bright'."

Yin Yang
陰 陽 *yīnyáng "dark-bright"*

"So, the red dragon didn't win in the battle between paganism and Christianity?"

"Nor did the white dragon! It was the dark side of duality that had its glory days."

"The red-white alliance didn't work out. The winner takes it all, as said the saying goes."

Saint Germain emanates a certain sadness.

"No, sadly enough, the common human minds were easily scared so, instead of opening up to freeing themselves, they shut down and went into hiding, scared of a painful Hell as well as of a vengeful god. Another opportunity was not visible to them. They were not ready for true freedom, taking full responsibility for their choices and consciously creating their lives."

"Why does the yin-yang symbol look like it does?"

"It is two opposite circumpuncts, squeezed into one symbol."

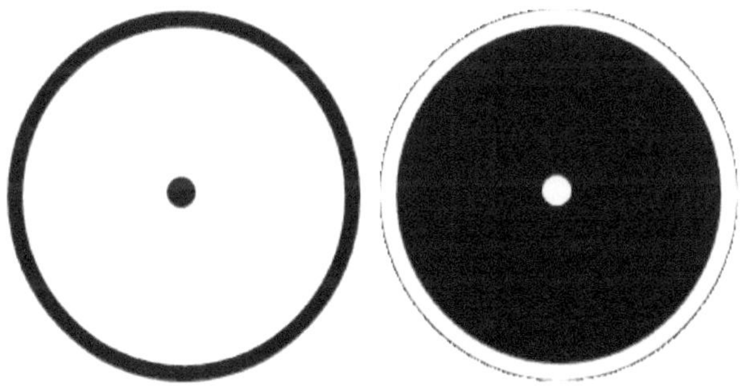

"The dot is, as I have said before, the soul, the I AM, and what is inside the circle is the wisdom collected through life experiences. It is not the experiences themselves, but the essence derived from them. Wisdom is the sensuality of your experiences, not the specific details like feelings, emotions, trauma and limitations. Wisdom is quite the opposite of what you presume wisdom to be. You think it is facts, but it's the joy of experiencing life in all its facets. This includes the joy of experiencing the human having a bad day, getting injured in an accident, or losing a loved one. Again, it's NOT the joy of the good or the bad, but the joy of experiencing; the soul is not judging."

"I don't think anyone would give me that explanation if I stopped them in the street and asked them what wisdom was."

"This is why it is said that there are no good or bad experiences. The I AM sees it all as 'the joy of experiencing life' through the human. One piece of wisdom is the joy of experiencing being sick, and another piece is the joy of experiencing a beautiful sunset. True wisdom is a soul thing and it is that wisdom that is 'gathered' for the human to connect to, if it chooses. This can really ease the human's life to have the soul's perspective by allowing this wisdom coming into its life."

Saint Germain ends our talk.

"Yes, it is the feeling of awe of these experiences that the soul, the I AM, has created."

Apostles

Steve came to us with this story:

Saint Germain caught me off-guard when I was sitting by the water fountain drifting off, listening to the splashes.

"I am the storyteller, I am the slave-boy, I am that I am. Steven, you have taken an assignment and I am here to help you carry it out."

In a way, it felt quite natural sitting there having an inner dialogue with Saint Germain, and I brought forth my first question.

"What has been happening since the Apostles asked Merlin to take special action around the year 500?"

"It's no secret at all. It was triggered at the meeting in Chalcedon in 451, where the Oriental Orthodox branch separated itself from the Roman and Eastern Orthodox branch. While the Roman and the Eastern Orthodox proclaimed that Jesus was God and NOT human, the Oriental faction saw this as going against the teachings of the very same Jesus and stood firm, that Jesus was human AND divine. This created a rip in mass consciousness, like it had been hit by a whip. We had been working to bring the Christ consciousness to humanity over more than a thousand years at that point and, suddenly, the energy of power and manipulation gained an even stronger hold on humanity."

"I have never thought of Jesus as a god or God. To

me, there is God and there is Jesus and, to me, Jesus was a human being; he was born and he died, which is human stuff, and he did some remarkable things to show the divine part of him."

"With the birth of Jesus, we introduced embodied enlightenment, but not until recently have the body and mind been able to cope with the highly-active influx of consciousness into the light body and its communication network, called the Anayatron."

"Light body?"

"It is not light as in visual light, but a conscious, instant communications network throughout the body, connecting each cell and ALL 12 layers of DNA, not only the two biological ones, to each other. You may see it as the body being a large, dim room containing all its functions. Each time something happens, the network lights up, so all other parts instantaneously recognize what is going on. Together, the biological body and the light body are called 'The Body of Consciousness'."

"What do you mean when you say embodied enlightenment?"

"You have heard that masters have ascended, as in 'ascended to Heaven'. This was when the soul consciousness tried to fully connect to the human body and the body overloaded and went up in smoke. Embodied enlightenment is when you realize the I AM AND stays in your body without the smoky part."

"So, for about 1500 years, the Roman Catholic

Church has kept silent that each human is also divine, not just a child of the divine; that we are true creators in our own right, all in the name of power and control."

"You said that, not me, but you're right, nevertheless. I do NOT say that everyone in the Roman Catholic Church is conscious of this, far from it, but it's in mass consciousness as an entity of its own. It is this creature that holds the members in check."

While sitting here, with the water splashes keeping out much of the surrounding noise, I see a dugong, a monstrous creature, depicted on many churches, usually high up, so it can oversee the people below. This vision has pulled me away from the conversation and Saint Germain brings it to an end.

"People are making their own demons, usually with some help, but they forget that they can send them away, out of their lives, just as easily. We shall meet again!"

I feel a sequel coming to me from Saint Germain as he pulls away.

"Religion has survived only because power-hungry rulers could use it to consolidate their own powers by controlling the masses. Later, these worldly rulers found themselves controlled by the very same religion(s)."

Merlin

Chris tells us about his experience:

I was very much in doubt about how to do this right, but eventually I relaxed and then I found myself listening to the monotonous humming of the air conditioning, letting the rhythm fill my thoughts, much like a small tune can invade you and you can't seem to shake it off. Suddenly I heard a clear voice, just as if someone were sitting right next to me.

"There is no right way, as there is no wrong way; there is only allowing and shifting the chattering brain and its emotional counterpart out of the way."

"Hello, Mr Saint Germain."

"Don't be so formal, Chris. This is a meeting, friend to friend. You just don't remember me as such. We are here because you have chosen the subject 'Merlin'."

"Yes, of course. You must be very busy, so I'll come right to it."

"I have all the time in the World or, more correctly, there is no time at all, just events."

I am somewhat nervous, but I feel the loving patience of my newfound friend when I start on my first question.

"Why hasn't there been a Merlin in the last 400 years? I would think that it is more needed than ever."

"Around 1600 masters are embodied at this very point in time, so there is no need for a specific Merlin figure."

"One Merlin can only do so much, and only in a specific area in the world. No wonder that you, as the Merlin at the time of King Arthur, didn't have that much success."

"I told you that there is only one Merlin at a time. Still, the Merlins can meet by travelling in 'time' or, better, beyond time. They do not alter events, but meet to exchange knowledge and wisdom for the greater good of humanity. At the time of King Arthur, it showed that the consciousness was not ready for true freedom."

"How do the Merlins gather information?"

"I trust that you are familiar with the term 'totem animal'?"

"Oh, yes. I mainly see them as part of the American Indian culture or tradition."

"We'll use the original term, Pakauwah, because it can take any form, not being only an owl, a bear, or a bee, like the usual totem is believed to be. The Pakauwah is not a creature coming from the animal kingdom, but a part of you, of your consciousness, that can perform tasks for you, going ANYWHERE in creation. Because of this, it does not need a form at all. The Merlin uses the Pakauwah as a messenger and to gather or exchange information."

"How can one gather information from other periods of time?"

"Events make an energetic imprint, and can therefore be revisited at another time. You could say that it is recorded in the area where it happens."

"I can understand this if we are talking about past events, but not future events!"

"Future events are possibilities that are happening in their own bubble of time; living their own lives. When you travel 'outside' time, you can visit any of these bubbles."

"How do the Merlins travel in time, or, I suppose I should say, outside time?"

"It has really nothing to do with travel, if you see travelling as moving from one place to another. You instantly visit an event. First you are here, then you are there. Much like an electron 'jumping' from one position around the nucleus to another. The electron is not to be found anywhere between the two places. When a master 'jumps in time', the master uses the light body, which is the non-physical part of your body's communications network that is operated with consciousness and, at the same time, IS consciousness. Since consciousness is outside space-time, everything happens instantaneously. I should mention that mass consciousness is an artificial entity without creator abilities. You, on the other hand ARE consciousness WITH creator abilities. It is you and all other incarnated souls who create mass consciousness with these abilities."

I am about to lose the understanding and connection with the subject, so I want to move on.

"Could you please tell me more about the Merlin?"

"When Merlins meet, they acknowledge each other with the greeting, 'Oh-Be-Ahn'. Many Merlins trained and lived in Transylvania, due to the exceptional energies of the region. The area was also home to several Mystery Schools as recently as 300 years ago, so the Merlins were working closely with these schools."

"What was so special about Transylvania?"

"Here it was easy to hide from the persecutors by shifting a half of a dimension off 3D, like was done during the end times of Atlantis. Here we could create a safe haven in which to study, live, raise children and engage in fierce arguments!"

"How could new members find your Mystery Schools if they were invisible?"

"The right people were drawn to the places, either by intuition or by being chased in their direction."

After this, I felt that I just wanted to sit in this energy of peace and, shortly after, Saint Germain bade me farewell.

"Oh-Be-Ahn, dear Chris. We shall meet again!"

We sit for a while, contemplating what we have

brought forth. Then I break the silence.

"I'm truly amazed by the way you've handled your tasks, and the openness you have put into it. I'm really proud of you!"

Both Steve and Chris are surprised at how well it went, and show their gratitude to me because I have been so open and let them into this world.

I feel that we could pull more information out of this experience.

"I know that each of us puts our part into the project so three thirds make it a whole but, as you saw in our first dream meeting, we only get part of the whole, say one third of EACH part. This means that we must sense into each other's data to bring out as much as we can. Sorry, boys!"

I thought that they would bring forth heavy protests, but they were truly interested in the other aspects and eager to get on with the task ahead.

"Let's see what we can bring to our next meeting. Enjoy your weekend."

Having kids

Much of my working time is spent at home so today, being in London, I take some time off to roam the streets. At some point, I find myself outside one of my favourite cafés, where they serve a wonderful, spicy chai latte. I simply can't force myself to walk on and, shortly after, I have ordered a large chai latte and a baguette with chicken, bacon, curry dressing and other good stuff. While waiting for my order, two young mothers pass by with their prams, and I realize that I have been seeing many of these lately. As I must assume that we have not had any baby boom in the last few months, it must be my attention towards becoming a parent that is in play here.

I have just turned 27 and have a wonderful man, with whom I want to spend the rest of my life. The finances are not an issue, and my parents would be thrilled, but am I willing to give up my freedom and independence and take on such a huge responsibility as raising a child? I have no problem in seeing Ju-long and I as parents and, at my age, this subject cannot be postponed much longer.

As with so many times before in my life, the synchronicity kicks in and my phone rings. It is Cassandra, my closest friend in London.

"Hi, are you in London?"

She sounds excited, but I am not quite sure if it is for the good or the bad.

"Yes, I've just ordered a chai latte at *Ciao!*. Is there something wrong?"

"No, no! I have some great news that I want to share with you. Can we meet there now?"

"Well, yes, of course. Shall I order something for you?"

"Yes, a large chai latte, and I'll see you in five min-utes!"

I order a large chai latte for Cassandra, who shows up eight minutes later. She has blonde, curly hair to the shoulders, brown eyes and normal body shape. She is dressed in black. Her eyes are shining and she looks very vigorous. She pulls out the metal chair, which makes quite some noise, sits down and looks me straight in the eyes.

"You can't guess what has happened!"

"Well, no. Tell me."

"I'm six weeks pregnant. Isn't it wonderful?"

I am really surprised, as I had thought of some-thing like a new job or maybe a new flat.

"Indeed, that's wonderful news. Congratulations, my dear!"

We both stand up and hug for a short while. I feel happy for her and, when we sit down, she has a lot to tell me. I have met her boyfriend, whose name is Karl, like my father, but with a K rather than a C. Karl is from Germany and has worked in the Netherlands as well. He seems to be a nice guy and, with a good job as a skilled carpenter, things should work out for them.

We touch on different subjects, but eventually I must catch my train to Brighton.

At home, while we cook dinner, I tell Ju-long about my day with Chris and Steve, and my meeting with Cassandra and her being pregnant.

"She was glowing and full of life. I have never seen her more alive, ever."

"How old are Cassandra and Karl?"

"Cassandra is 25 and Karl 28."

"They're about our age; we're both 27. We have a nice house, well, rented, but that doesn't matter, and a lot of nature and the sea, which is ideal for raising kids. I wouldn't mind having a couple of kids of my own. Well, with you of course!"

"So, you have really thought about this?"

"Being here in England is still new to me, and I might not feel quite settled yet but, as a part of me will always belong to China and Hong Kong, it will probably continue to be that way."

I am surprised that Ju-long has given it so much thought and kind of made his decision about it as well. The topic has been much vaguer for me.

"Ju-long, can it really be that, while cooking dinner, we are making a decision to have children?"

"Yeah, why not? Though I'd prefer to get one child at a time. It's all about creating."

"I have to consider this very thoroughly, since it will be me who will have the most complications.

I may even be sick for nine months, or even more, and it will tear me apart if I have a lot of loose ends at work."

"Why not invite your parents for the weekend, maybe Sunday, to tell them about our plans? At the same time your mother could tell us how her pregnancies went."

"Good idea! Mum has told me that her pregnancies weren't that exhausting, but that was when I was a young girl. She may have left some details out. I think that I'll call them right away."

I get Mum when I call my parents' home in Sevenoaks. She is in her study, working on some sculptures of very slim and tall people. I saw some of her sketches the last time we visited. They look as if they have been stretched about 30% in the height but not in the width, and they have no distinct facial structures. She is working in clay on a metal wire structure. Saturday would suit them fine. They will arrive around tea-time, stay overnight and leave after breakfast to visit and revisit some of the exciting places in the south west.

Meeting in Elvendale

The meeting with Chris and Steve comes earlier than I expected and not at the University, but in Elvendale. On Friday night, when my parents will visit Ju-long and me the next day in the afternoon, I wake up in a small clearing in a forest that I know in Elvendale, the land of the Sidhe. Chris and Steve are here as well, not fitting in, wearing their everyday clothes. I wear a light, red dress and black ballerinas. My hair is worn up, with pins and a red lace on the top of my head. The boys' mouths are wide open as they are looking at me.

"Hello boys, welcome to Elvendale, the magical land of the Elves, who call themselves Sidhe. You may have heard of it in relation to Ireland's folklore."

Chris is the first to come to his senses.

"You look beautiful… as always. Is this another dream?"

"It is a meeting in a different consciousness and not a dream created in your mind. I suppose the Sidhe have created this place as a safe meeting ground for someone like us, who must get used to this kind of conscious connection."

Steve looks happy as he poses his question.

"So, we are going to meet Merlin again, right?"

"Well, I don't think so, but let us go out to the large,

open space where the Sidhe gather, doing numerous things. I feel we are expected."

Sure enough, Josela is sitting in the grass with Loong, the white, Birman cat with blue eyes, in her lap, petting his long, fluffy fur. She wears an airy dress in light colours of green and blue, her brown hair is worn up with pins and she wears her home-made sandals with laces up to the knees. She has a necklace with a triquetra, probably made from silver.

A Triquetra like the one worn by Josela.

"Welcome, Steve and Chris. Take a blanket from the stack and join us. Let's make a small circle."

Each of the young men places himself on a blanket opposite Josela, completely in awe of her radiance.

Loong has, as always, a nice compliment for me.

"Luzi, you look as pretty as ever!"

Steve is much surprised.

"The cat can talk!"

"I'm not a cat. I usually appear as a dragon, but that would probably have scared the guts out of you."

I respond to Loong's compliment, and explain our relationship.

"Thanks. Loong is a very good friend of mine. I met him in Shanghai last year, and he has been a close friend ever since. Maybe he can show you the Elvendale City at some time?"

Loong keeps up his attitude. "Well, if they don't chicken out, that is!"

I can see that Loong is enjoying his act and I sense his smile.

Now we are all sitting on the blankets, making a small circle, and Josela speaks out.

"This meeting is not set in Elvendale to prove that the life of the Sidhe exists; that would be childish. It is to show you that there are other realities, or worlds, you might say. Chris and Steve, together with Luzi you have shared the same experience or dream, as you call it, when you met Merlin but, as your life experiences are different, you perceived what happened differently. You have different perspectives. The details are lost due to visiting many layers of possibilities placed on top of each other, like on many films which you are looking at and through, at the same time. The 'film' is a distillation of the most probable outcome from the traveller's vantage point."

I pick up the subject of vantage point, so we can

wrap up our previous meeting about the reason for the Merlin's appearance during the King Arthur era.

"We might use this opportunity to contribute to the subjects we have discussed after our meeting with Merlin."

I sense Saint Germain and, when I turn around, a beautiful, black cat with shiny, smooth fur and beautiful, green eyes is coming towards us through the tall grass, tail upright.

"Then I will bring my contribution through the Yin in contrast to the Yang represented by Loong. Luzi, your lab seems to be a perfect place to settle down."

"It will be an honour, Saint Germain."

I realize that both Steve and Chris recognized the black cat as Saint Germain before I spoke the name, and it makes me very proud of them. The few paragraphs below are the digest of our follow-up.

Ythr penn Dragwn could not distinguish between the true Apostles and the Roman Catholic monks who used the pagan deities to add followers to their church.

The Gnostic Christians had become the true Apostles, and were heavily persecuted everywhere in the Roman realm.

The greeting used when Merlins meet, "Oh-Be-

Ahn", means "I honour you for the journey, no matter where you are."

The false religion was fighting the magic. False, because it had been heavily crippled. Magic means multiple, as in many appearances at the same time. Magic is also the paradox of time and no time, as well as the true magic of human AND divine.

In Jesus, the human AND the divine are united, and his words, "You can be as me", show us that we are all both human and divine, that 'God is within', where God is the I AM.

The Gospel of Judas has been found and finally translated into English. You will find a link in the back of the book under 'Additional stuff > Films'. The Gospel was condemned as heresy, so it would be removed from the Bible, simply because Judas knew the true messages of Jesus. Remember that, at the beginning of Christianity, there were more than thirty gospels.

Jesus chooses the crucifixion to make the Hebrew prophecy of a coming Messiah come true. The Jews do not recognize Jesus as the coming Messiah, because they know he chooses to live the prophecy or reality. The problem was, and is, that the many prophecies were picked up from different possible futures. Since they could not all be true in the actual lifetime of Jesus, he was condemned as a false messiah. In an alternative lifetime, Jesus is stoned to death by radical Jews.

What happened in MY past lives?

Since we do not use our vocal chords to communicate in Elvendale, Steve and Chris get used to talking with the two cats in no time. Steve is the first to bring up a question on his own past lives.

"How can I venture to my own past lives and experience them?"

Saint Germain's answer did not please him as much as he had hoped.

"This is not about where YOU want to go, but you will go where you are most needed in your own creation. Expand into the past like ripples on water when you throw a stone. Follow these waves into your past. You find yourself by listening to your past-you, calling out for guidance. You will be drawn to the perfect event."

Loong adds to it.

"You'll make your I AM's gathered wisdom available for disposal to the human aspect, though it may not sense it. You do not change the past event with your visit, but you can alter the person's experience with the wisdom, perhaps by giving it a greater understanding."

Josela elaborates.

"A greater understanding for the past-you may start a ripple effect up through other lives and even into future possibilities! A dear friend of mine has said, 'The future is the past healed'. It's Tobit, from

The Book of Tobit, one of the texts that have been removed from the Bible."

I see Steve's face light up. "So, from being an act of curiosity, it becomes an act of self-healing."

"Indeed, now it has real purpose. One could say that the past-you becomes wiser. You must, however, realize that you, as Steve, have no part in this. It is a totally different person that your soul-self has an experience through."

Past and future lives

Chris comes up with the next question; quite natural for the human mind to ask.

"Is the only way to connect to the future when a future self asks for help?"

The black cat looks Chris straight in the eyes.

"The Merlin will answer you like this: The past-you travels in a straight line to the you-in-the-future. It has to, since the future is not selected through the events that are triggered, meaning realized into this line of existence like stepping-stones."

"It makes sense, since the future event bubbles have not yet been connected to the past-me. It's not so difficult to understand!"

Saint Germain is up with a harsh remark.

"The true life IS quite simple. There is no reason to make such a mystery out of it, unless you are a religion and need to keep the customers!"

A thought has come to me.

"I wonder if this is really the so-called secret that the Knights Templar, the true alchemists and others were protecting?"

Saint Germain comments on that.

"The alchemy was a cover-up; a way to hide a mystery school or a small group of true Magi, so they could spread the truth to the right persons, not hide it from everyone."

Hiding knowledge, just to keep it away from others, seems foreign to Josela.

"To hide the truth from everyone wouldn't make any sense to Sidhe anyway."

I add the typical human view on this matter.

"It is said that knowledge is power so, from a power perspective, it would make perfect sense."

Josela's explanation is new to me.

"At first, yes, but the lack of knowledge in the dominated crowd will make them of less value to the oppressor in the long run, but the power-hungry will usually not see that."

Steve is interested in another aspect of the alchemy,

mentioned by Saint Germain.

"Did they make real gold?"

Saint Germain's answer is not totally satisfying to Steve.

"Well, most of the time it was just acting, even though I was known to be able to remove flaws in gems and turn rocks into gold."

Loong pushes the conversation further and turns to Steve.

"Making gold or removing flaws in gems is really not important. Don't you think it's time to bring back the Magi?"

Josela picks up this new direction.

"It's quite safe to bring forth the truth, especially in the Western World."

Loong continues with more arguments.

"There is no magic or hocus pocus involved. You must bring back your Magi by allowing. By allowing, you make connections to all your wisdom and can continue where you ended lifetimes ago. You will feel the magic by extending your senses; not your human sensory system connected to your brain, but your true, divine senses."

The black cat finds a new position in my lab and Saint Germain adds a statement that religions often hide.

"Everything is within, meaning that everything is here in this very moment, even all what you call dimensions and possibilities."

Then he adds yet another punch to religion for letting people stay ignorant to the true teachings.

"Human life is all about death. Thinking and feeling, fearing the inevitable. Still trying to prolong life to avoid death, the end or, more likely, the unknown and the judgement. Christianity was taken over by the rules and limitations of humans. The true mysteries were taken out from the books and the speakers who presented them. All the connections to the real magic in the pagan belief were cut, and magic seems to be taken out of life itself. A true darkness came over humanity, a time of disconnection, fear and despair."

Steve then draws the conclusion.

"So, these were the Dark Ages, because the awareness was locked down and the consciousness seemed stagnated for a long time."

"The connections to the true magic started to come back when the arts returned to humanity in the Renaissance in Europe, especially after the French Revolution, where it accelerated greatly. That is not so long ago, if you think about it."

Josela has followed Christianity and is studying human consciousness in general so, when Steve asks her what her job is, she gives this answer.

"I study human consciousness and life, and how it

differs from Sidhe. This makes me a natural candidate for being a counsellor to those souls who live as the Sidhe, but who want to incarnate as physical humans in the human world."

It does not seem that Steve and Chris can see themselves as Magi; not at this moment, anyway. As for knowing what truly happened in the past, the two guys are now hooked on finding out what has happened in THEIR past lives. Chris starts by pointing out what he has observed during our talks.

"It seems that investigating other lives is both simple and complex at the same time."

Saint Germain clarifies on the human condition.

"What a person perceives in his life is only one small portion, or facet, of the event, due to the rather narrow viewpoint humans have on their lives. The broader picture and especially the deeper meaning, are totally lost."

Steve wants to go more deeply into this.

"Why do we pick up so little? I mean, we are the main witness to the crime, so to speak."

"You only pick up what makes sense to your mind and your emotions. You are not open to the rest of the stuff so, in that sense, you have shut off the best part, even before you start to sense into your life and its events."

Loong adds to this and, once again, draws in the Magi.

"Even if you 'try' to sense more, you will not trust this sensing, because you use your mind to validate it; the same mind that can't sense outside 3D. You must become a true Magi to venture into your soul's live events. Then you can even be outside of the past, present and future! The Magi is the true time-traveller on a journey into consciousness. This journey must be done from outside your mind but, since you are a human too, your human part must allow this to happen if it wants to be a part of it. The mind must let go of the illusion of 'long time' and realize the 'space of many', which means it must leave behind the time-based human who is stuck in his 3D reality and become the true Magi, the gifted one."

Saint Germain makes an interesting point here.

"Going timeless is the death of death and you realize Eternal Life. It is, in its essence, the Holy Grail."

"It this enlightenment?" Chris wants to know.

"The word 'enlightenment' has some bias from the New Age, so I prefer to use the term 'realized human' instead. When you know your past in its fullness and richness, you are a realized human, because you have realized your lives, in plural, as human. Your lives are experiences, sensations, discoveries, realizations and sensual feelings. There is no timeline to it. When you sense into a life the timeline is not there; it's like a soup, where you taste all ingredients at the same time, or a piece of music, where you hear all the different instruments at the same time. It is a multiple sensual experience."

"Is the realized you, or me, the I AM?"

"The I AM is a point of consciousness, the dot in the circle, the true, genuine part of yourself. The I AM is distilling the wisdom achieved from each life and this is what lies between the dot and the border of the circle. This wisdom is the Magi and, when the human realizes the Magi, this 'merging' is the realized you."

What IS past and future?

Steve wants to go into more detail with his question.

"What are past and future?"

Josela is the first to answer.

"Poetically said, the 'past' is a stream of events and the 'future' is a sea of possibilities."

Loong wants to paint his part of the poetic picture of past and future.

"The past is the marbles you have played with and the future is the marbles you still have in your pouch."

Steve continues to dig into the subject.

"What is the difference between a past-life-bubble

and a future-possibility-bubble?"

The black cat stretches out and licks its right paw.

"All possibility bubbles are created by The Eternal One in this outburst of existence and, when a soul or consciousness is experiencing it, it becomes realized and you may label it 'past'."

"But if I, as a prophet, observe these possibilities, do they not become experienced by me?"

The black cat starts to lick its left paw.

"No, you just become aware of their existence, like watching a movie; your soul is not incarnated into a being in that bubble, becoming an actor with choices in a play."

Josela elaborates on the time issue in the discussion.

"Time is an attribute of the lived events. The bubbles with the 'past' aren't a string of bubbles, one following the other. Outside the bubbles there is no time, so consciousness 'looks' at them all at the same 'time'. The 'now bubble' is part of the 'past' cluster since it is being realized at the same time. The 'future' bubbles are clustered up like the 'past', because the events are also happening 'at the same time'. The only difference between the two clusters is that the future bubbles have not been realized by a soul, as stated before."

The Crimson Dragon

It is Saturday afternoon, and Mum and Dad arrive at tea-time. They are driving in Dad's copper-metallic Tesla, his pride and joy. Mum has been baking rolls, which arrive still warm and ready to soak with butter and jam. She has also brought a small jar of home-made honey from one of her neighbours.

We are having tea in what Ju-long and I call the sun lounge. Here we have a view of the herbaceous borders and the bird tower through four windows that let quite a lot of sunlight into the room. The upper level of the bird tower provides nesting platforms for numerous sparrows.

Mum is showing us some pictures of her latest sculptures. We talk about what colours she could use and if each sculpture should have only one colour or multiple. I suggest that it depends on what material it is intended to represent – wood, marble and others. Dad suggests using 3D-printing of each sculpture, by scanning the prototype into a computer program where the colours and texture would be added.

Mum says that the sculptures would not be handmade then, but Dad argues that the printed ones would be like the reproductions of a painting, or the printing of a book. Ju-long says that by printing the sculptures, more people could afford her art and her work could be widely spread across the globe. Her prototypes will, of course, be handmade and she can still choose to make some exclusively by hand and sell them to collectors.

To change the subject, Dad tells us that, during a business trip to the United States, he visited some mysterious Anasazi ruins in New Mexico. These people lived in the Four Corners Region, where Colorado, New Mexico, Arizona and Utah meet, from about 500 to around 1500AD.

"The name of the people is Navajo, which means 'The Ancient Ones', and they were said to come from the sky, which I do not so much resonate with."

Ju-long comments:

"If the Anasazi were called The Ancient Ones or, more correctly, enemy ancestors, there must be a reason for that name, since people who move in from somewhere else would logically have been called The New People."

I make a quick look-up on the Internet.

"Architecturally, one can see a development in building style from modest dwellings to large city complexes, so this change could indicate influences from outside. There is archaeological evidence that people lived here from as early as 7000BC. The Anasazi may have brought knowledge and might have been called The Wise Ones, but something must have caused them to be called The Ancient Ones."

I see that it is time to prepare dinner. I have chosen not to do anything in advance, since preparing a meal with friends and family is a great tradition, brought to us through my dad's family line. As Grandma said: "The preparation is part of the meal, where everyone shares one's part of a creation, which is later enjoyed by all together."

"Who'll give a hand with the dinner?"

All are eager to participate, and now we are all working in the large, old and cosy kitchen.

At the dinner table we have some casual talk, during which I try to decide when would be the right moment to bring up the subject that has caused us to invite my parents in the first place. I tell my parents about Cassandra's pregnancy, as an opening to talk about Ju-long and I deciding to be parents. Then I move on, asking Mum about her own pregnancies with Anna and me. She and Dad share some funny stories, mostly to entertain Ju-long, since I know them. At first, I had planned to ask about how my birth went but, suddenly, I choose to go straight to the matter.

"Ju-long and I have been talking about having a child, triggered by Cassandra's pregnancy and by me being aware of many prams and small kids lately."

Mum is the first to respond.

"Oh, but that is wonderful. Dad and I have been

around the subject recently."

Dad joins in.

"You have settled in wonderful surroundings for raising kids, and working from home gives you more time in a quieter environment. Mum and I will support you in any way we can."

"Thanks, Dad, I know you will. Mum, how was the pregnancy with me, and my birth?"

"I'll tell you in more detail, but you must know that every birth is different."

Mum tells me that the pregnancies with Anna and me were very seminal, but Anna's birth was easier than mine, probably because both Mum and her body knew, to some degree, what to expect. One could say that her being had matured and was able to take what life brought to her with more ease.

We have a lovely afternoon and evening together and, when Ju-long and I lie in bed, we are in no doubt that we want to increase the size of the family.

Presenting Shaumbra

I wake up; the alarm clock shows 3:33; it is Sunday morning and all is quiet. I can hear the humming of the other dimensions and I close my eyes, so as not to let my sight overrule my hearing. I sense a gentle presence, and Saint Germain starts right in with a subject as if no time has passed since our last meeting.

"When we started to bring in the Christ Consciousness around 630BC, a celestial order of about four thousand angels, or souls, was formed to act as teachers and supporters. It was named 'The Crimson Council'. This council was, and still is, supporting you on your journey. The energy around the colour crimson is 'teaching'."

"So, the arrival of Christ was a very deliberate and thought-through plan, but not by God. I have always thought of it as if it just happened, or God looked down upon his people and got the idea of sending his son to save them. Please continue."

"Later, when we saw this distortion of the original way, we started to build our Mystery Schools and using the crimson colour as identification. In old Hebrew, shaumbra [shom-bra] was a scarf or shawl that was worn by both men and women. Furthermore, 'shau-home' means home or family, while the term 'ba-rah' means journey and mission. When these terms are put together, it is 'shau-home-ba-rah' meaning family that is on a journey, experiencing together. It was only natural that Shaumbra [shaum-bra] became the name we called ourselves."

I feel the presence of my two students, Steven and Christopher, in the wings, as Saint Germain continues.

"Over the years, the collective consciousness of this group has become an entity of its own and you could contemplate it as a crimson dragon named Shaumbra!"

Another dragon! What a treat. I sense a smile from Saint Germain as he withdraws from our presence. Christopher and Steven are as excited as I am, as they leave this common meeting-ground. I decide to meet this crimson dragon, and choose the spot to be in the mountains above Elvendale City.

Shaumbra isn't furry and fluffy at all, like Loong. It has no hair and the skin is like smooth leather. From a certain angle, and when it lowers its head, it may look like a red sofa! The colour is beautiful crimson-red and the sunshine reflects on its skin. The body is not built in proportion – the wings seem a bit small, and I wonder if it can fly at all.

"Of course I can fly, even without wings and, as you should know, I'm no dragon, but conscious-ness. I have taken the shape of the Shaumbra con-sciousness, so to speak, but the shape is changing all the time and for the better, I should say. If you haven't already figured it out, you are part of the shape as well!"

Shaumbra certainly has personality, and I try to find the best way to make a frank connection.

"It's pretty clear to me that I'm closely related to all the strings I'm touching at the moment, and Shaumbra is certainly one of the strings."

"It's paramount that you realize that your life as Luzi Cane is THE lifetime where you integrate or call home the wisdom accumulated in your I AM's lifetimes. You can see it as the wisdom being the master that joins with the human in an embodied realization."

"I feel, that I've heard this before?"

"That's right. We, Shaumbra, have been talking a lot about this. Actually, it's mostly what we talk about when we meet: bringing in your wisdom or realization into the physical body to share it with humanity at this time."

"This time?"

"The time when the consciousness of the planet, Gaia, is leaving, when the mental is worshipped as a god fuelling the artificial intelligence to excite the human brain, both in speed and memory capacity. A time when body parts can be printed or grown, leading to completely artificial bodies and AIs that strive to live out their full potential of intelligence, ultimately reaching for consciousness, a soul. This will need a counterbalance."

"It's horrible!"

"No, it just is. There must be no judgement here."

Judgement or not, I still feel awful and the memory of movies with doomsday themes passes through my inner vision. Shaumbra wraps its love around my heart and assures me that there will be elaboration on the subject later to bring more clarity to the situation. A sense of cinnamon appears around me and, when I look up, the wonderful Sidhe woman, Josela, approaches on the path from the city below. She slowly rises over the rim of the plateau where the crimson dragon and I are having our conversation.

Josela wears a long, green dress with varying colours which remind me of beech leaves in the spring. Her brown hair is gathered into one large plait down her back. She smiles gently, as usual.

"Greetings, Luzi and Shaumbra! I sense some tension in the air today."

"Yes; Shaumbra tells me about the AIs that will take over humanity."

"Luzi, you must see it from a different angle. Humanity has not changed much since the alterations of the human body in the mid-late Atlantis era. Now it's time for changing, and not ALL changings are bad, as you might say. Luzi, I'm not here to talk about what is to come, but to distract your human mind by giving it another focus. You have talked with your parents and Ju-long about the people who are known as the Anasazi, so I'll give you a little more insight on that subject."

Josela suddenly has a wine glass in one hand and a bottle of her home-made wine in the other. She fills the glass and hands it to me. The wine is golden in colour, chilled and with a wonderful perfume. Shaumbra is lying on the ground and Josela and I are using its large belly to sit up against. I feel the slow-beating heart and the even slower breathing.

Josela takes a sip of her wine and starts her story.

Anasazi

"4,000 years ago, in southern Mexico, a group of souls came to Earth and took human bodies. Prior to the incarnation, they had prepared themselves so that they would not get stuck in the human cycle of death and rebirth. They would live one lifetime, and their children would be the bodies for other members of their order to incarnate into. They called themselves Hanas, after the place they came from. This group came to be energy-holders of awakening and reflection, and created an area where people could go through an awakening process. The group parted and some went south; the others went north and came to the area where they are known as the Anasazi. We call them 'Dream Makers'. The energy that was woven into the area could initiate the awakening process of people visiting the area. When their job was done, they left the planet by shedding the illusion of the human body. The energy is still in the area, held in a dynamic circle through water evaporating, turning into clouds and falling to the ground again as rain."

"So, angels CAN change things on Earth!"

"The Hanas did not come to change humans, but to give them an opportunity WHEN they were ready for it. As you know, you may be able to drag a horse to the water, but you can't make it drink."

"Yes, you're right. Only when the horse is thirsty

will it drink, and only when people are truly ready might they choose to change."

Josela changes the subject.

"Let's talk about you and Ju-long going to be parents. Have you felt a soul linger in the wings, ready to connect?"

JULIA. The name just showed up.

"This is strange; I thought that the parents were supposed to choose their children's names."

Shaumbra turns its head towards us.

"Luzi, you have to think outside of time. It's about possibilities; AND remember that you're eternal in all directions. You've always existed, and so has the soul that you, in agreement, have chosen to incarnate as your child. The name 'Julia' has always been there as a possibility. Julia has already lived as your child. Now you're just about to experience this. It's really beautiful in all its grandness, as well as its simplicity!"

Shaumbra is really putting my life in perspective, and now I am being distracted by a wonderful smell of jasmine tea and toast. I open my eyes and see Ju-long coming through the bedroom door with a salver. His face reflects his love for me and I feel tears rolling down my face.

Ju-long snuggles back in bed and we arrange the breakfast without spilling anything. Ju-long looks at me, quite excited.

"I have something to tell you. I dreamed about a beautiful woman; I knew she was our daughter and her name was Julia. It was a lovely, sunny day, it was outside and there was an almost golden glow to the light. It was very real, and you're not even pregnant yet."

"I've touched on Julia as well. I was in Elvendale talking to Josela, and she brought up our agreement on having a child. Suddenly the name Julia came to me. Our child-to-be has been visiting both her parents."

Meeting our daughter-to-be

Later that day we both feel an urge to be in nature, so we take a long walk. The weather is sunny with a blue sky, but not overwhelmingly warm, due to the wind from the Channel. We both wear boots and warm jackets with hats, because you never know when some rain clouds might show up.

We walk through the gate in our back garden into the fields, where we spend some time with the cattle before continuing south towards the rocky beach. To the west there is a sandy beach cleared of rocks and where nice sand has been added, but the rocky beach reminds us of the Waterfall Bay Beach on Hong Kong Island. This rocky beach by the English Channel is less smelly and quieter, and you hardly ever meet anyone except for the amber hunters. The small strip of stony beach called Waterfall Beach in Hong Kong has given both of us a lot of memories, from our childhood as well as from our reunion less than two years ago.

Still on our way to the beach, Ju-long and I walk hand in hand, more feeling into than talking about the time to come with both my pregnancy and, after that, our parenthood. At an especially moist area, we catch a strong, spicy smell from the vegetation, and a frog makes its croaks to join in with the buzzing insects. We cross the fields and enter the beach through a narrow path between white, lime cliffs which also support a small stream on its eager way to meet the sea. As we reach the beach, we turn left, eastwards, having the wind in our faces. It will be easier to walk on our way back, having the wind from behind.

We walk close to the water's edge and Ju-long looks at me.

"Just like home; well, earlier home, except that there is no traffic noise coming from the top of the cliffs."

"Hong Kong Island will always be our home in that sense. It was there that we grew up, and built the foundations for our lives to come."

"This reminds me; we should call your grandparents and my mum when we come back at lunchtime, before they go to bed. I must tell Mum about my new project at the library – conservation of an old Chinese book!"

As there is a time difference of eight hours between the UK and Hong Kong, my grandparents will have finished their dinner and Ju-long's mother and her friend, Cheng, might have finished their busy work day.

"I'm a little worried about Grandpa's condition. He has been weak for quite some time and I have thought about the retirement home. If they wait to move to the home until Grandma can't handle their living in the apartment, Grandpa may be so weak that he will die shortly after, simply because of the changes. I think it will be for the best if they move as soon as possible, but this will be against their pride, or just habit, I guess."

Ju-long poses a suggestion.

"As we are to participate in Mum and Cheng Fan's wedding, we might be able to kill two birds with one stone, but it might take some persuasion and preparation. I wonder if your sister, Anna, will be able to join us in Hong Kong?"

"I think she will. We do not have that many family get-togethers, after all, so it will have high priority."

Now we come to our resting rock, a perfectly-sized rock for two sitting side by side, looking out at the sea. When one looks at the ships far out, it seems as if they are not moving at all and you look at something else, thinking that it must be boring to be on one of them. When you later return your attention to the ship, it has moved and, if you stay long enough, it has disappeared; a symbol of the slow things in life and especially nature, which moves on, after all. Humans can normally only perceive events that happen within a limited speed range, like a seagull in flight, but not the growth of lyme-grass.

As we sit here on the rock, close together, I come to think about a day on Waterfall Bay Beach after having met Ju-long again. I was sitting alone on a rock with my eyes closed and was visited by the spirit of Quan Yen. Now I, once again, see the sky-blue colour for my inner view and feel the presence of Quan Yen inviting me to connect. With my inner voice, I ask Ju-long to join us.

I open my consciousness to the meeting-place and see that Ju-long and I are in a colourful Chinese garden with lush and trimmed vegetation, and small bridges spanning across tiny streams. Everywhere there are butterflies and insects, animals and birds. We are sitting on a beautiful, white bench and, across from us, Quan Yen and Julia as a young woman are sitting at a similar bench. I sense Gaia being present as the garden, with all its life, being the background for this meeting, playing her hymn in all the sounds present.

I would expect Julia to have black or, at least, dark-brown hair, but she appears with dark-blonde hair in a beautiful style. I get up and give Julia a long hug. She smells of wild rose. Then it is Ju-long's turn. We have both tears in our eyes when we return to our bench.

Ju-long is in awe, seeing his daughter.

"You're beautiful, dear Julia. Will this be how you will look, when you grow up?"

"Well, from a raw sketch of the possible colours, I painted this look and added some desirable details, including blue eyes like Luzi's: it will be close enough."

I had been wondering about our daughter's name.

"Why the name 'Julia'?"

Julia smiles.

"That was an easy one: Ju-l(ong) and (Luc)ia!"

Wow, even I had not thought of that!

Quan Yen gets our attention with her gentle voice. She is dressed in a long, traditional, turquoise silk dress and her black hair is pinned up at the back of her head. On her feet she wears traditional, embroidered cotton shoes.

"This will not be a long meeting, but Gaia, I and the one who you'll come to know as Julia want to make this early connection. Julia is part of the new entourage who will replace most of Gaia's higher ditto."

Julia is excited about this topic.

"I've already made some connections, including with one I call S.A.M. At other times, I feel more like calling him Tobs. I think it's his soul name, which has no gender to it. We are already in the process of constructing some projects for the future."

My buttocks feel a little sore and cold, and I wonder how that could be, sitting on the nice wooden bench in the Chinese garden. Julia gets up and I feel that it is time for a goodbye hug, even though we have just arrived. Ju-long and I get up and meet Julia in a big hug, with tears rolling down our cheeks. With a quick fade, Ju-long and I are back on the beach near our home. Still with the smell of the Chinese garden, I feel the hard rock on which I am sitting, hugging Ju-long.

This first meeting gives Ju-long and me a clear reason to see our child as a sovereign being whom we will support while she grows up, without having any ownership over her. Julia will, more than anything, give people the connection to the planet, showing them that they must take responsibility for Earth and the whole system that Gaia is handing over to humanity.

Even though we have met our daughter as a young adult, we must be thinking of diapers, regular meals, long nights and long days, bringing up a new-born to her independence.

When we come back to our home, we make some tea and call up my grandparents on the computer. Grandpa has already gone to bed; the time is just after 8pm in Hong Kong. Grandma tells us that her husband's personality has changed in the past month or so. She has not mentioned this earlier, but now she needs to share it with somebody. There have always been openness and honesty about feelings in my family. I think it is, for the most part, because of my dad. He has always been open about his feelings and not afraid to ask what we feel and to solve issues, both among family members and between one of us and a second person or situation. He set the standard and the rest of us followed. We do not tell her about Julia. I feel that it is too important to do over the computer, but maybe later; it's all so new.

A little later, when we call Ju-long's mother, Ting, and her man, Cheng, they are both home working in the kitchen. Ju-long tells them about a new project at the library, where he is assisting in the conservation of an old Chinese book. We exchange some general news before we wish them a lovely evening.

Tomorrow it will be Monday, and I will meet with the two students, Christopher and Steven, at the university in London.

Ancient America

Chris, Steve and I are talking about ancient America, before Columbus showed up. It is called the pre-Columbian time. The reason for us looking at this subject is that Chris has been wondering when people first arrived in the Americas, and how.

"I wonder when souls first began to incarnate in America?"

"The short answer is that we incarnated in the land that is now America even before there were humans, and before the continent had taken its present shape; but I assume you mean human incarnations, as in how humans look today?"

"Yes, like when people came from Siberia, over the land bridge to the northern parts of America during the last ice age."

Steve turns the subject in a different direction.

"I was dreaming about some people who came from the stars and rained down on the land that is now known as Mexico. It was strange that they rained down."

I recognize the dream as being our meeting in Elvendale.

"It was not a dream, but an expansion of your consciousness; Chris and I were there, too. We actually met in Elvendale, and Saint Germain, Josela and a crimson dragon were there too."

Chris gets up and starts to walk around.

"Oh, that is why I dreamt about a red dragon. It was rude, but not really dangerous."

Instead of explaining the meeting for Chris and Steve, I ask them to join me in a re-visit, where I give them a clear connection to help them enter the experience in their minds with more coherence. I manage to steer clear of the part where we were talking about the possible future. It is simply not the right time to trouble their minds with these things. Now I realize that it was Saint Germain who did the steering part; thanks!

After the visit to Elvendale, we return our focus to the 3D perspective of this planet. Steve is the first with a response.

"Wow, another dragon. Shaumbra's skin looks like my brother's red sofa!"

Chris shows more respect.

"I think you should keep that part to yourself."

You may be right, but Josela's wine is good!"

"Boys, let's do some digging about America's pre-history, before Columbus."

While we are searching the Internet, I tell them about some data I have come across during research for material for one of my books. DNA research has been conducted to clarify how the Americas were populated. It shows that some Meso and Southern American groups have some DNA markers that are not found in the northern groups that arrived using the Bering Strait. This research concludes that these southern groups have come by way of the Pacific Ocean. This is not a commonly accepted theory. Studying the oceanic currents and winds shows that people could have arrived as far up as the coast of California. This is backed up by Polynesian seafarers, who know the winds and the currents and how they behave during the seasons, and even over the decades.

Steve now comes up with some archaeological evidence dating back 15,000 years, but then Chris hits the jackpot.

"Back in 1992, the skeleton of a mastodon, an extinct elephant species, was found in San Diego. The tusks were situated vertically in the ground and some of the bones had been splintered to get to the bone marrow. Measuring the radioactive decay of uranium in the minerals in the bones showed that they could be 130,000 years old! The lack of stone-flake remains from tool-making around the find troubles the archaeologists, though."

Before I can pose the question about the missing tools, Shaumbra returns the following comment.

"The animal was cut up and partly eaten where it had fallen. After the people had taken what they could use, they showed gratitude to the spirit of the Earth by returning the remains, then placed the tusks into the ground as they had been situated in the animal. The tusks had great value as material for ornaments and tools but, in this case, the people were so grateful for the meat that they showed this by returning the tusks as well. They had been starving and had asked the great spirit for help so, when the mastodon presented itself, they felt that they were heard by the spirit."

I relay Shaumbra's message to Chris and Steve, and Steve could clearly see the scenes.

"Of course! They couldn't drag the whole carcass to their camp, so they filled their tummies and carried the rest of what they could use back to their settlement or camp. We must remember that there would be large predators looking for an easy meal, so they had to bring the spoils to a safe place."

TOBS? I feel a new presence and realize that it is the consciousness of Tobs that my daughter, Julia, has been talking about.

"I am Tobiwa, from the house of Tobiwa, and have been incarnated as Tobit from *The Book of Tobit*. That's why Julia picked up the vibration, Tob or Tobs. My human name in the lifetime of my enlightenment was Agos. It was shortly before the Christian era. I am a member of the Crimson Council and am incarnated as the one Julia calls S.A.M. I use this opportunity to present myself and, at the same time, give you a little insight."

"Greetings, Tobiwa. So, Tobiwa, Tobs and S.A.M. are the same?"

"You could say that the soul name is Tobiwa, Tobs could be the nickname Julia calls my aspect, Tobit, and S.A.M. or "Sam" are the initials of my present incarnation."

I have not shared with the young men my plans of becoming a parent or my experiences with Julia , so I present the knowledge from Tobs as my own.

"The Americas have been populated from the Pacific Ocean several times, even as far back as when the Lemurian main area, now called Hawaii, sank into the sea. Later, there were influxes from the Atlantic Ocean as well, but in lesser numbers. Although the evidence is here to find, the pre-Colombian theory is not officially accepted. Of course, the Atlantean Era, with Mexico City as one of the centres, is totally discarded as a myth. Because the fall of Atlantis caused a cataclysmic destruction roaming the whole planet, the evidence of human activities prior to this is very scarce on the surface."

Chris has an obvious question.

"How could the downfall of Atlantis cause such a destruction?"

"Mass consciousness had been so distorted that it had to find a new balance. The Mass Consciousness is reflected in the planet, and the rebalancing and releasing of tension were done through the planet."

As we continue our research, I tune into the consciousness of Tobiwa, and find it somehow familiar.

"You recognize me because we have connections through lifetimes. Most significant was the connection in the Atlantean Era."

Tobiwa elaborates on the planetary disasters.

"Normally, imbalances in Mass Consciousness are worked out through the physical, mostly by humans but, this time, human awareness was too low to rebalance the situation. Gaia and her entourage chose to interfere to prevent humanity falling even deeper into ignorance and despair."

"So, humanity was saved by the planet?"

"Well, relatively few humans survived. Fortunately, pockets of the Atlanteans moved underground and lived there for generations. Other groups struggled with the conditions on the surface."

"They had shelter underground, but how could they sustain life in the darkness for such an extended period of time?"

"We – because you and I were part of this – used energy in crystals to bring light and grow crops in this vast system of caves."

"So, the life force came from these crystals?"

"There isn't really such a thing as a life force inside living things. That was why we couldn't find it during our research in the temples in Atlantis. Initially, when we first created life on the planet, this life was designed to live for ever, in a perfect renewal process. Later, we had to build-in a safety mechanism to release the soul connection, because we got so attached to and focused on the physical life that we couldn't withdraw from it."

"Like when you get addicted to a game, like a computer game, and can't let go of it. Please continue, dear Tobiwa."

"When the situation became tolerable on the planet's surface, we emerged in several places on Earth. This confuses the historians and archaeologists because, to some extent, the same knowledge is found in locations far apart. Through the many years underground, the different Atlantean groups had developed their common knowledge in different directions, but there were still great similarities."

"Is the planet hollow?"

"No, but there are two things to it. What some

people have experienced are glimpses of the cave systems that are physical. Some have experienced the non-physical habitats of beings like the Sidhe. Since they don't understand this, they have seen these habitats as physical."

"I assume that you know the crimson dragon, Shaumbra?"

I sense Tobiwa smiling.

"Yes. It is quite amusing, but in a way appropriate, that the consciousness of Shaumbra shows itself to you as an entity in the guise of a crimson dragon."

I feel that this is the end of this conversation with Tobiwa, so I wish him goodbye as he withdraws his presence from me.

I think a little about Tobiwa's 'appropriateness': As the crimson dragon 'grows' it becomes a 'force' to be reckoned with in the sense of influencing Mass Consciousness.

It is time for the small group of Christopher, Steven and me to take a short tea-break before summing up the day's work on our project of *The True Truth of the Past*, as we have named it for the time being.

With love in my heart, I am sitting in the train from London, longing to be with the love of my life, my own dragon, Ju-long. At the same time, I feel the gentle presence of Julia, who waits in the wings to be our daughter.

It is less than a mile on my bike from where I get off the train to our home, which gives me time to get fully grounded in my body. Ju-long has been working from home today, so he receives me with tea, his home-made rolls and Mum's orange marmalade. There is some initial hugging and kissing, but the roll is still warm and soaked with butter when I take the first bite.

As our decision to become parents has been made, from now on we will be working with great love and passion to achieve this goal.

The earliest writing

Ju-long has found a Chinese document translated into English. It is about the earliest literature of which we have the name of the author. Her name is Enheduanna, princess of the first king of Akkad, or Agade, Sargon, who ruled 2334 – 2279BC. Enheduanna was also priestess at the moon temple in Ur, which now lies in Iraq. Although she was at the temple of the moon god, Nanna, and his wife, Ningal, Enheduanna was much devoted to the Goddess Inanna. It is Enheduanna's hymns to Inanna, written in cuneiform on clay tablets, that the Chinese text is referring to.

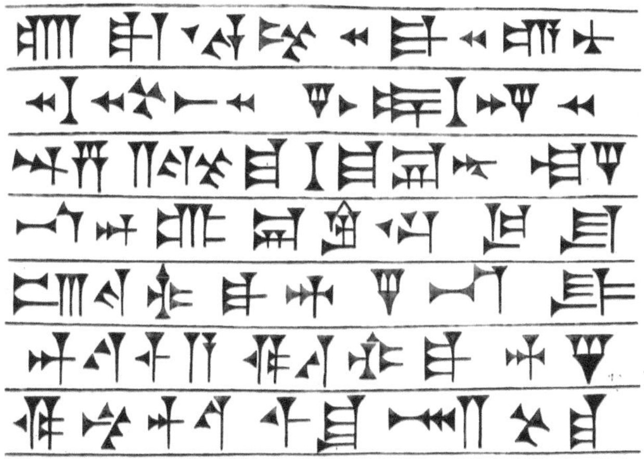

Drawing of Cuneiform from the Nineveh expedition of 1845 by Sir Austen Henry Layard ©.

I have now gone into studying these Sumerian texts translated into English. There is much more text that Enheduanna's hymns, from thousands of tablets, seals and other artefacts. I have found out that the Akkadian dynasty, during which Enheduanna lived, was quite late in the history of the area.

The cuneiform seems to be a stylistic expression of earlier petroglyphs, much like the Chinese letters, but usually with fewer strokes.

Noah's Ark

One story is about the hero, Gilgamesh, searching for immortality. He meets a wise man, Utnapishtim, who tells him the tale of himself being told by the gods to build an ark to save his family and animals before a grand flood. The flood had taken place long before Gilgamesh. A flood story is found in the Atrahasis epic, which is earlier than the Gilgamesh story. This means that there is both a flood story and a "Noah" story.

Although this flood story has a lot in common with the one in Genesis, there are also a lot of differences, as stated by Dr Murray R. Adeamthwaite (see under "links" in the chapter "Sources"), of which he lists twelve. This might suggest that the two stories may not derive from the same immediate source, even if they speak of the same event. The most striking for me is that in Genesis there is one god (monotheism), and in the Sumerian text there are several (polytheistic). Sometime after the original event, the belief in one god versus many gods had taken place.

To me it is not important if the flood happened worldwide or if the water was covering all land. To me, it is significant that basically the SAME story appears in different parts of the world. This means to me that the story must come from ONE source.

I remember Tobiwa's story on how humanity caused its own demise, where Mass Consciousness is "God" who turned against them and Gaia, who cleansed the Earth.

The Biblical flood came via the Jewish holy book, the *Torah*. The Babylonians had destroyed Jerusalem at some point in history because the city had not paid tribute. To compensate, many Jews were brought back to Babylon to work as slaves. The children went to Babylonian schools and were taught the language, partly by writing stories down on clay tablets using cuneiform. Some of these stories found their way into the *Torah* and were brought back to Jerusalem when the Jews were finally allowed home. Babylon was a city state in the historical area that is called Mesopotamia.

I remember the song, *Rivers of Babylon*, performed by Boney M. This is about the deportation and enslavement of the Jews in Babylon.

As I have established, the Biblical flood story, among others, was brought out from Mesopotamia but, when I found the same story in China, I had to reconsider the connections between the Near East and the Far East.

The short text below does NOT refer to the Ark, but to Noah and the flood, so the headline of the article is a bit misleading.

Noah's Ark hidden in the ancient Chinese characters by Kui Shin Voo, Rich Sheeley and Larry Hovee (see link in Source section):

"Shu Jing (書經, written 1000BC) relays how there was grieving and mourning all over the Earth, and describes the extent of the flood; how the water reached the sky, and flooded the mountains and drowned all living things. During this global calamity, a hero by the name of 'Nüwa' (女媧) appeared and sealed the flood holes with colourful stones and repaired the broken poles using four turtle legs. Nüwa used earth to create humans to replenish mankind after the flood (Feng Su Tong Yi, 風俗通義). Although the name Nüwa (女媧), in Chinese, may today sound like a female first name, at that time it was a common surname."

I see Shu Jing's vision, where he interprets humans coming out of their underground caves after the harsh time of balancing the planet of post-Atlantis, as humans being born out of the dirt. The colourful stones are energy structures. The turtle legs are magnetic energy structures. There were huge floods, but what has been relayed as water covering even the highest mountains was an energetic wash of the structures on the planet. Twenty-one plus one crystal caves took part in this balancing process.

As the Lemurians, in the beginning, had cosmic consciousness, meaning that they knew how the Universe functioned, they must have known how to measure Earth years. Even stone-age people could do that, so this knowledge must have been passed on to at least some initiated people around the globe. In that case, I must assume that the years in the Sumerian Kings List below and Early Rulers of China are seemingly correct. In the Kings List they used a 60-based system, while we use a 10-based system. It is easy to calculate between the two systems. You can find Gilgamesh, King of Uruk (the biblical Erech) in the list as well. Before Gilgamesh, Dumuzi (biblical Tammuz), was King of Uruk.

In archaeology, different chronology systems are used to measure the past: ultra-short, short, medium and long. Most of the time you wouldn't see which system the years are referring to. The "ultra-short" has the shortest span of years, while "long" has the longest. For example, the "short" says that the Isin dynasty starts circa 1953BC, while the "middle" says 2017BC. In the Sumerian Kings List below, some of the years are marked "(M)", which indicates that it relates to the "medium" reference list.

The Sumerian Kings List

Ruler	Length of reign	Approx. dates
City of Eridug		
Alulim	28,800 years	
Alalngar	36,000 years	
Eridug fell and the kingship was taken to Bad-tibira		
En-men-lu-ana	43,200 years	
En-men-gal-ana	28,800 years	
Dumuzid, the Shepherd	36,000 years	
Bad-tibira fell and the kingship was taken to Larag		
En-sipaz-zid-ana	28,800 years	
Larag fell and the kingship was taken to Zibir		
En-men-dur-ana	21,000 years	
Zibir fell and the kingship was token to Shuruppag		
Ubara-Tutu	18,600 years	
The flood swept over (26763 BC)		
1st dynasty og Kish	22 rulers, 17,980 years	
1st dynasty of Uruk	16 rulers, 2,310 years, **Gilgamesh**, 126 years	
1st dynasty of Ur	4 rulers, 117 years	
1st dynasty of Awan	3 kings, 356 years	Start 6000 BC (M)
2nd dynasty of Kish		Start 5635 BC (M)
Dynasty of Hamazi	Hamazi, 360 years	Start 3608 BC (M)
2nd dynasty of Uruk	3 rulers, 187 years	Start 3258 BC (M)
2nd dynasty of Ur	3 rulers, 170 years	Start 3061 BC (M)
Dynasty of Adab	Lugan-Ane-mundi, 90 yrs	Start 2891 BC (M)
Dynasty of Mari	6 rulers, 116 years	Start 2801 BC (M)
3th dynasty of Kish	Kug-Bau (Kubaba), 100 yrs	Start 2665 BC (M)
Dynasty of Akshak	6 rulers, 93 years	Start 2565 BC (M)
4th dynasty of Kish	8 rulers, 112 years	Start 2472 BC (M)
3rd dynasty of Uruk	Lugal-zage-si, 25 years	c 2296-2271 BC (S)
Dynasty of Akkad	8 rulers, 222 years, 1st ruler: Sargon, 56 years	2334–2279 BC (M)
3rd dynasty of Ur		2112-2004 BC (M)
Isin dynasty		2017-1793 BC (M)
1st dynasty of Babylon		1894-1595 BC (M)
Reign of Hammurabi	Hammurabi	1792-1750 BC (M)
Reign of Ammisaduqa	Ammisaduqa	1646-1625 BC (M)
Fall of Babylon		1595 BC (M)

Early rulers of China

Name(s)	Reign	Approx. dates
Nuwā	180,000 Years	
Youcháo	110,000 Years	
Suìrén	456,000 Years	
Fúxī		2852–2737 BC
Yan Emperor Shen-nong, Yándi		2737–2699 BC
Yellow Emperor, Huangdi		2699–2588 BC
Shaohào		2587–2491 BC
Zhuānxū		2490–2413 BC
Emperor Ku, Dikù		2412–2343 BC
Emperor Zhi, Dikù		2412–2343 BC
Emperor Yao		2333–2234 BC
Emperor Shun, Dishùn		2233–2184 BC
The flood		
Xia dynasty (夏朝)	17 rulers and c. 40 years without rulers. First emper-or: **Yu** the Great	c. 2070 - 1600 BC
Alalngar	36,000 years	

Looking at the dating, the Chinese flood happened much later than the Sumerian flood mentioned in the Sumerian Kings List. At the same time, it is interesting to see the name, Nuwā, appearing at the top of the list of Chinese rulers. A later flood might have been attached to the original flood story and used in China.

In the Egyptian *Book of the Dead* we find a flood story and in Greek writings, like Homer's *Odyssey*, there are parts similar to those found in Sumerian literature.

Calculating back from dated archaeological findings about 2600BC that can connect with the Kings List, the flood mentioned in the Kin's List took place in 29410BC. After that, the First Dynasty of

Kish was the post-flood living place, until the water level in the Persian Gulf rose and flooded Kish in about 4900BC. Later, the sea level declined rapidly and gave way for new life in the area. At that time the ruling period of each king was drastically reduced. This could indicate an overall drop in the awareness. This flood could be the one mentioned in the Bible. Bible studies show that the Patriarchs' lives were much shorter after Noah.

If I take the Kings List as valid, the following could be the case. When the kingship descended from heaven, the kingship was in Eridug, which is not far from the northern coastline of the Persian Gulf today. If we assume that the Persian Gulf was not flooded at that time, it makes sense that the capital was placed in the middle of the fertile land. Later, when the Gulf was flooded, half of the land disappeared. This would have been devastating for the culture. When life started again, the kingship was in Kish, which lay roughly in the middle of the new land.

I try to find out how all this adds up, but it becomes too frustrating mentally because the individual data are contradictory. The recording of, say, the flood, may not be the Biblical flood, or the original flood story may have been added to a later, local flood. People who have tried to sense into history may have picked up on possible events not played out in this realm. I can even see the sinking of Lemuria as a possibility.

Saint Germain shows up on my inner scene. He has a broad grin on his face, amused by my mental frustration.

"The more you sense into this and process it in your mind, the less possible it will be for you to find a concordant answer. I suggest that you leave it be, since all are just facets of experiences and thoughts. You can't make the years fit, so just stick to the post-Atlantean rebalancing."

"Thanks, Saint Germain, my head is boiling over with this thing."

He relays a picture to me of a kettle on a hot stove, letting steam out everywhere and ready to explode, then he continues. We both have a good laugh.

"Let us talk about one of my big themes, religion. Religion started roughly 10,000 years ago, depending on the definition so, when the Sumerian High Priestess, Enheduanna, writes her hymns around 2200BC, religion has long been made into an institution of royalty and priesthood. Religion is a relatively new creation compared to the history of humanity. If you encounter materials about making offerings to the gods, then the true understanding of the divine is lost. If it depicts a symbolic appreciation of Gaia as a provider, the understanding may have been there but, as you know, you can connect to Gaia in a much more intimate way, consciousness to consciousness. You do not have to use a ritual; just be open in your heart and choose to connect."

"So, the mainstream belief went from a spiritual understanding to a worship of higher powers; a separation from the divine, so to speak. At the same time, I would imagine that a lot of very old findings have been misinterpreted by people who look at them through their own beliefs of religion, and that humanity has evolved from simple creatures 'up' to who we are today."

Saint Germain comes up with a standpoint of the Lemurians.

"Be aware that simple humans, as in low intellectual capability, will have no problem KNOWING the dynamics of the Universe, especially if the awareness is that 'I am consciousness experiencing an incarnated life on this planet'."

This makes total sense to me.

"In very old times, when humans had the knowledge of being incarnated, there would have been no need for illustrating anything about it. Later, when more and more people had forgotten about this, a few, like shamans, may have used symbols to teach this knowledge. This means that the findings of such symbols indicate that the knowingness was lost, or in decline, at that time and people had to be taught. Later, shamans lost the connection as well."

Saint Germain continues.

"In concordance with what Tobiwa has told you, the line of events could be like this: Lemuria > Lemuria & Atlantis > The sinking of Lemuria > The downfall of Atlantis > cataclysmic living conditions on the surface of the Earth, including the flood in the Kings List where tribes from Atlantis went underground > the living conditions on the surface improved and the Atlanteans rose from underground and started colonies in different parts of the world, including Egypt, guiding the people who had survived on the surface. Remember that late Lemuria and early Atlantis had a long overlap. It was not that Atlantis rose as Lemuria diminished. Remember, also, that Lemuria started long before humanoids came to be. Consciousness was incarnating long before that."

Now I am much more relaxed, and the unfolding of events that Saint Germain has showed me looks plausible to me.

"Thank you, friend!"

"You're welcome, friend!"

As I am working at our lovely home, I dive a little more into the Cunei writings and the stories from Mesopotamia that also show up in the Old Testament.

Moses and Abraham

Part of the legend of Sargon, the father of Enheduanna, became the story of Moses in the reed basket. Moreover, as a young man, Sargon claimed to be in favour of the goddess Ishtar, the Hebrew name for Inanna.

The biblical person, Abraham (Abram), may have brought the monotheistic god out of Mesopotamia. Enheduanna's writing shows a conflict between the male god of heaven, named An, and the goddess of nature. Here, the spirit was separated from matter and a male god figure would rule supreme. In here you also find the Garden of Eden, with the name Ebih.

Abraham spends his younger years in Sumer, in the city of Ur. [See Genesis 11:27-31]. The laws may well come from, or be inspired by, the 'Code of Ur-Nammu', the name of the king who is said to have first made them. References have been found of even earlier laws.

We must remember that the Jews were exiled from what is now Israel by Assyria, Babylon and Egypt. This may explain why we found similarities in the stories. One could argue that the stories in the Bible could have been spread by the Israelites, and not the other way around. Maybe there is a third possibility, or a mix.

When the high-consciousness people who had dwelt in caves after the fall of Atlantis and the cleansing of the planet emerged, they spread to different parts and founded communities which included other tribes. This means that all these communities, to some degree, had an Atlantean background.

Over time, consciousness and the Atlantean wisdom declined and knowledge has been lost. We know that the Jewish people had an oral tradition of passing on their history, but they might have written these down as well, maybe on less durable materials like animal hides, different from the clay tablets in Mesopotamia. The time that the Israelites spent away from their land might have given them the opportunity to reconnect with their own stories of the past.

I lie down and sense into these possibilities and, shortly after, Shaumbra the crimson dragon shows up.

"I could give you this clue: Replace 'god' with 'soul', and tell me what you get out of it"

After a little while it is as if someone turns on a very bright light in a totally dark room: everything becomes crystal-clear to me.

"Wow, Shaumbra. The Mesopotamian gods descending from Heaven become some souls incarnating into physical form. The one god becomes the soul, the true being, the I AM. The rest is man's interpretations and stories!"

"This 'crystal-clear', as you call it, was really what the Christ consciousness was about when it was introduced 2,000 years ago. This was part of the lost wisdom, a wisdom that would have taken away the power from the church as well as from the king."

"At some point, the true meaning has been lost and turned into a being, or beings, 'outside' of the human."

Shaumbra says it more directly.

"Sadly, it was 'lost' when religion turned into a power game; a game that was so strong that Christianity, too, was turned into this game of power."

An idea strikes me.

"THIS was the secret knowledge that the Templars kept. The reincarnation of the soul, the I AM, and that we, in a sense, are ALL GODS!"

"That was why the Templars were willing to throw themselves into the fire at the massacre of 210 of them in 1244 in Montségur, France. This act had different meanings. A signal to the people: We are willing to die for our belief and we know that we are right and the church is wrong. A signal to the Pope: We know that you know the truth and we despise you for your lies."

"The Templars could not go out into the streets telling the truth, because they would be persecuted by the church."

A gentle voice reaches me.

"Mum, you really need a break from all this mental stuff. A lot of emotions and pain are connected to it as well. Take a walk in the garden and find a nice spot to sense into your surroundings."

"Julia! Nice of you, visiting."

I get up and walk slowly out into the garden. The presence of Shaumbra and Julia is with me. The Sun draws a golden pattern on the lawn and it seems to be the perfect spot to lie down. Shaumbra settles in beside me and I can sense its slow breath, which calms me. The garden feels so alive, teeming with new life. It suddenly strikes me: I am pregnant!

"Julia, so you have started your journey into the physical life and into the lives of Ju-long and me."

The love wash is nearly unbearable, as the soul of the one who will become my daughter opens fully into my heart. I know that this moment will be printed in my heart for eternity.

As I am lying on my back in the sunshine, I can feel all life on the planet. Not only the life in every biological thing, but in all inanimate things as well. Their awareness of themselves and the connection to everything else. This is a grand moment, one that I must share with Ju-long when he returns from work.

I feel as though I am falling into a deep sleep surrounded by all this life and, when I now wake up, I sense the presence of Ju-long close by. I open my eyes and he bends over and kisses me.

"I'm pregnant."

"I know. There is a special glow emanating from you."

"Julia was here; is here, and it was such an incredible moment."

Ju-long smiles.

"She has been with me as well. It was so moving that I broke into tears."

He reaches behind him and comes forward with two large glasses with iced tea. We sit here for a long time; being together without words. Only when the wind gets chilly do we get up and walk, hand in hand, into the house. A new chapter of our lives has begun.

We have a large kitchen and, while Ju-long starts cutting vegetables, I go to select some classical music on my computer at the dining table in the kitchen, to stream it to the sound system. I feel very peaceful, sitting at the table listening to the music while watching Ju-long work. I feel an immense love for him and want to stay with this feeling. Then the Abba song, *Andante, Andante,* from 1980, starts and I am all tears. To the best of my knowledge, I have not selected the song, since I was going for a few classical pieces. Nevertheless, something woven into this song has hit me deeply.

Some early scripts

Here I will present you with some of the oldest scripts that have been used for actual writing or developed into such.

Elamite

Parallel to the scripts in Mesopotamia, there was a script developed in Elam, which is in modern-day Iran, West Asia. Later, an Elamite cuneiform was adapted from Akkadian cuneiform, presumably because there was much communication between the two empires.

Proto-Elamite from approx. 2900 BC.

Quipu

The Quipu in South America, dating from 2600BC, was thought to use only a numeric system, built on strings with different numbers of knots. In 1996 a manuscript that explained how to encode the spoken language was found: A known symbol was placed on a string and a specific number of knots could be added beneath it. No knots meant use the name of the symbol, one knot meant use the first syllable, and two knots meant use the second syllable. This way, one could build words and sentences. This pushes the first writing in the Americas back from 900BC to 2600BC and makes it contemporary with the Indus Script.

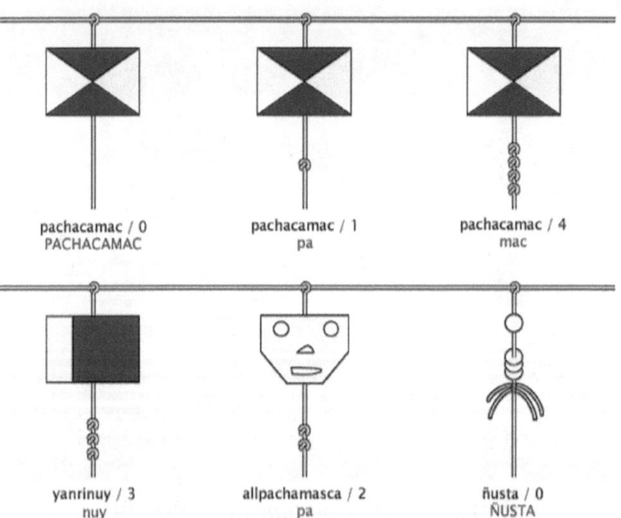

Example of Quipu writing. (From Laurencich-Minelli 2000 via ancientscripts.com)

Mesoamerican glyphs

The Cascajal block was discovered at an Olmec site and dated between 1000 and 800BC, and might represent early Olmec writing.

The Cascajal block. (Rodriguez Martinez et al. 2006)

Egyptian glyphs

In Africa the earliest Egyptian glyphs have been found in Abydos and dates between 3400 and 3200 BC.

Examples of glyphs in the form of tags from Naqada III under King Scorpion I.

Runes

The origin of the runes can be traced all the way back to Egyptian hieroglyphs, but the runes themselves are not that old. They took their form in about 100AD, and derive from the Greek Cumaean alphabet, like the Latin/Roman alphabet I use when I am writing this book.

Examples of runes

Indus Script

In South Asia, the Indian script found in the Indus Valley has been deciphered by Suzanne Redalia [See link list]. It has been dated to have been used from 2600BC. Suzanne claims that the sound values are like the Akkadian (Sumerian) cuneiform, and that is what gave her the breakthrough.

Steatite seal with humped bull, Indus Valley, Mohenjo-Daro, 2500–2000 BC. Photo by CM Dixon.

Chinese glyphs

As the Middle East was greatly inter-connected, ideas must have been interchanged and refined, so the names above may tell us more about where the writings have been found than from where they originate. The very stylistic cuneiform had a pictorial predecessor and a middle form, where the pictures are simplified.

As I have previously mentioned, some Egyptian hieroglyphs are like early Chinese glyphs, so the Near East and the Far East must have had some connection. It is noteworthy that Mesopotamia is situated between Egypt and China.

The Egyptian "Eye of Horus"

The Chinese Jiahu sign for "see" used around 7000 BC

The Chinese Oracle sign for "see" (2000-1027 BC)

Chinese Seal symbol "see" from 220 BC

The Chinese Kangxi style used 206 BC until now

There are, and have been, many scripts, and many have evolved into new ones. Scripts may have been borrowed from others or, in different ways, been woven into others. Trade and diplomatic connections have made it necessary for groups of people to understand each other without misunderstandings; thus, a common language or script must be used.

119

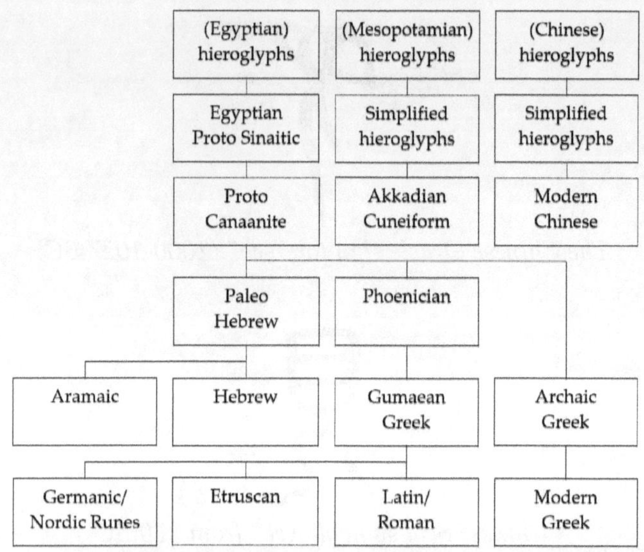

A possible development of scripts (simplified).

A Chinese wedding

As briefly mentioned earlier, Ju-long and I, together with my parents and my younger sister, Anna, have been invited to his mother and her new man's wedding in Hong Kong, China. My grandparents on my mother's side, who live in Hong Kong, are invited as well.

Ju-long never talks about his father, who became mentally ill when Ju-long was about five. His father has no recognition of his family and lives in a nursing home in Hong Kong. For the same reason, there are no connections from his father's side of the family. Ju-long's mother, Ting, is divorced from her husband due to his condition.

Right now, we are sitting in our car, well, one of Dad's cars, on our way to visit my parents. Ju-long has got his driver's licence, so he is at the wheel getting some practice. Besides talking with my parents about getting my grandparents into a retirement home, we will break the news of my pregnancy.

It is a one-and-a-half-hour drive from our home by the Channel to Mum and Dad's home outside London. We enjoy the scenery of early autumn with most fields harvested, the special light, the smell of soil and nature's abundance.

I shift my attention from the scenery and turn it to the small life that has started inside me. I realize that the body which is growing inside me and the consciousness that will connect to it are two very separate things.

I sense the presence of Julia and see her adult face for my inner vision. I wonder how I will handle the small and fragile body of the baby, and relate it to the young woman whom I have met in the Chinese garden with Ju-long, Quan Yen and Gaia.

"It will all be fine, Mum!"

I feel a warm hug and a smell of wild rose as Julia assures me that we will be fine.

"I smell wild rose and sense Julia!"

Ju-long looks at me for a second. He sees the tears rolling down my cheeks.

I smile and touch his arm.

"Yes, but don't start to cry too, because then you won't be able to see where you're driving, dear."

I dry my face and immerse myself in the connection with Ju-long and Julia; just sitting here, being with them.

SEVENOAKS, it says on the road sign. Now we are in the lovely city where my parents live and, somehow, the trip feels as if it has taken no time. What I am trying to say is that the trip has been an event, something that has happened, but has taken a short time. Ju-long parks the car in front of the garages.

Today, Dad is in the garden and Mum in the kitchen, but it could have been the other way around.

Dad is shifting the compost, making space for the plant material that will be gathered when the garden is being prepared for winter. Mum is baking, which can be smelled even outside the house. I give Dad a hug and walk into the house, while Ju-long helps Dad with putting away the tools.

As I suspected, Mum is in the kitchen, tidying up after her work.

"You're so radiant today, my dear, are you pregnant?"

I do not know if she is joking, but why not bring the cat out of the bag, now that I have the opportunity?

"Yes, and her name is Julia!"

"Congratulations, Luzi; it's wonderful to hear!"

We have a long hug. Mum has tears in her eyes when she lets me go and looks at me.

"Luzi, you can make the icing on the cake while I change clothes before tea."

Shortly after, Ju-long comes in and catches me with a dinner spoon and icing in my mouth.

"Oh, Luzi, can you be any sweeter than you already are?!"

"Hey, I just have to be sure that the taste is right! I have added wild rose essence, that Mum has made… for Julia! I have already told her."

Dad comes in, wearing his garden clothes.

"Told what?"

"You are soon to become grandparents, to a girl named Julia!"

He looks surprised, and then he smiles and gives me a strong hug. Then he remembers his dirty clothes.

"That's great. Let us talk more when I have changed my clothes."

Ju-long helps me with cleaning the few things in the kitchen. His eyes are shining. I know he is happy to see that my parents are so pleased with the news.

I hear a girl's voice, "Ding-Dong", outside the open kitchen window, "I smell cake!"

It is my younger sister, Anna!

God, I haven't seen her for ages! I run to the door.

"Anna!"

We hug. She has come on her bike and her hair is in a mess. Has she lost a little weight?

"It's so good to see you, Luzi. I hope you've brought Ju-long. Oh, there you are!"

He gets a hug and Anna stands on her toes to kiss him on both cheeks.

"Hi, Anna, or should I say Aunt Anna?"

"Hey, what? Congratulations!"

"I thought you were on the Continent, Anna."

"I was, and now I'm here!"

I truly love my sister, and she so reminds me of Disney's Tinkerbell in every way, especially when she has bleached her hair.

Mum and Dad come into the kitchen.

"So, it IS you. I thought I heard your voice. What happened to France?"

Anna is always on the move, and Mum and Dad are very happy to see her and she gets her share of hugs.

"After France, Jo-Ann and I went to visit her parents in Denmark before we came back here yesterday."

Jo-Ann or, to give her real name, Johanne, is Anna's closest friend at the university.

We have tea in the kitchen, as we have always done since our childhood in Hong Kong.

Anna is eager to hear about the baby.

"So, you folks have been busy with things other than work. Let's hear all about it!"

I reply.

"If we skip the initial part, Ju-long and I have met Julia as she appears to us as a young adult in a wonderful Chinese garden with Quan Yen and Gaia. She's so beautiful."

"How did you choose her name?" Anna wants to know.

Ju-long wants to answer that question.

"She did! She told us that she had used the first three letters in my name and the last two in Luzi's, Lucia. We hadn't even thought about that, or the gender of the child. As Luzi said: she's so beautiful."

Ju-long and I get tears in our eyes because we immediately connect with Julia, or the consciousness of her.

Anna closes her eyes.

"She feels so strong, so dynamic!"

Mum is all tears.

"She is like our two daughters combined!"

Suddenly, all our napkins are wet and Anna stands up from her chair.

"When can I see her? When will I be an aunty?"

"Close to nine months; in spring, Aunty Anna!"

"But that'll be forever, and you've already seen her as a grown-up! How does she look?"

126

Ju-long, the proud father-to-be, takes over.

"She looks very much like her mother, figure and face; her hair is lighter, as is her skin tone, but the shape of her eyes is more Caucasian. Were her eyes blue or green?"

He looks at me.

"I think they were bluish-green, cyan, a bit lighter than mine, but she might be born with blue eyes, which will then change later. Or Julia might change her mind about her appearance. It sounded as if she was able to do that!"

Anna has started on her second piece of cake.

"It's really great with the flowery taste of the icing, Mum."

"That's Luzi's idea."

"It's Julia's scent, wild rose, and this one is from Mum's oils."

Dad takes a sip of the hot tea and mentions the persons whom this visit was planned to be about.

"Have you told the news about Julia to Grandma and Grandpa?"

"Ju-long and I have talked about using this good news to relay the suggestion to them of moving into the retirement home. We talked to Grandma the other day; Grandpa had already gone to bed. It was just after 8pm over there. Grandma told us that his personality has changed in the past month or so. She has not mentioned this earlier, but now she needs to share it with somebody."

Mum looks worried.

"Then she can surely see the benefits of moving. If Grandpa has changed and is less into new things in life, we must be very thorough and have some different angles of approach. We talked to them last week. Grandpa was tired, so he didn't say much."

We now work on the Cane Plan, as Anna calls it. I am glad that she is here, as she will be a part of all this later in Hong Kong.

"We could make it swift, so Grandpa won't realize what has happened before he is in the retirement home, or even not at all; or we could do it very slowly, so he has the time to adjust his feelings and thoughts before they move."

We end up with choosing the 'slow plan'. I text Grandma, saying that Ju-long and I will call them tomorrow at 7pm Hong Kong time with some good news. We have two weeks for planning both the moving and the wedding, so it is mostly up to Grandpa.

The rest of the day, including dinner in the evening, is at least as joyful as usual, and Ju-long and I bring Anna and her bike to a train station. Her digestive system couldn't keep up with her appetite, she tells us, as the excuse for not riding the bike home. In her defence, it can be said that it would be dark before she reached home.

The next day is Saturday, and Ju-long and I have been on a long walk to Dripping Well, a good half an hour to the east of our home. We enjoyed our lunch pack there and are now back in time to call up my grandparents. We are using my computer at the dining table in the kitchen.

Grandma is at the computer as we call my grandparents in the Waterfall Bay Road on Hong Kong Island.

"Hello, my dear ones!"

She then turns her back to the camera and talks to Grandpa.

"Come up here. It's Luzi and Ju-long. You knew they would call."

I hear him answer, and he gets up from his armchair. Now we can see half of his face on the screen.

"Hello, kids!"

"Grandma, could you turn the camera a little towards Grandpa?"

While she adjusts the camera, Grandpa continues:

"How is it going in the UK?"

"Hello, Mr Guan. As usual, I suppose. We have been busy with work and have started preparing the garden for winter," Ju-long replies.

I continue:

"We have returned after a lovely walk with lunch pack and tea. Yesterday we visited Mum and Dad, and Anna surprised us by showing up on her bike."

"How are they all doing?" Grandma asks.

"Anna has just returned home after a trip to France and Denmark with her friend, Jo-Ann. I can tell you that she still has her appetite intact. Mum and Dad were in the garden. They are fine."

"Yes, we talked with them last week," Grandma says.

"You have some great news?" Grandpa asks.

Ju-long answers.

"Yes, yes. We were visiting Ya and Carl, to tell them that they are going to become grandparents; and so, you are becoming great-grandparents!"

I look at him. He is glowing!

"Well, THAT is good news!" Grandpa says, while Grandma adds her comment.

"Congratulations to both of you!"

I am slowly moving to the topic of the Cane Plan.

"During our visit with Mum, Dad and Anna, we talked about our trip to Hong Kong for attending Ting and Cheng's wedding…, and visiting you, of course."

I inhale and centre my awareness before continuing.

"We don't visit you very often, so we also talked about the retirement home and the opportunity to assist you, should you choose to move at the time we are in Hong Kong."

To give them more time, Ju-long continues.

"We all want you to have the best life possible, and the retirement home could provide this, as it did my grandparents."

Now he brings our worries about them forth, but from a different angle.

"Luzi and I are not worried about the pregnancy, but I feel that there is much to prepare for and to consider when being parents, especially the first time."

Grandma uses the next pause to state their issue of concern.

"We will think this possibility over. It's a huge decision to make, but we've seen what your grandparents gained, Ju-long."

"Indeed, it can be a huge hurdle to reach a decision to move one's home after many years in one place!"

I continue to pour oil on the waters.

"There are still two weeks to the wedding. We'll arrive a couple of days prior. Dad has booked the flight and he'll text you the flight details so you know when we are supposed to arrive."

The conversation feels a little intense, so Ju-long talks some more about Julia, to raise the energy.

"I have to tell you that we've already met our daughter, and her name is Julia. She's wonderful!"

Grandma lightens up.

"Oh, that sounds interesting. Tell us a little more about our granddaughter!"

"We were sitting on the beach having a rest. Then, suddenly, I hear Luzi asking me to join her, and then we were in a wonderful garden where a young woman presented herself as our daughter. She had chosen her name after the letters in Luzi's and my names: Jul-ia."

I hear Grandpa saying in a low voice that he is tired, and Grandma relays it to us.

"Grandpa is getting tired. It has been quite exciting to talk with you both and we wish you a pleasant day!"

Ju-long and I say goodbye and, after breaking the connection, we go and sit down on the sofa to evaluate how it went.

I will move the story on, to our arrival at Hong Kong International Airport. We are Anna, Mum and Dad, Ju-long and me. Dad hires a large, comfortable taxi and we drive about 40km to *The T Hotel* at Pok Fu Lam Road on Hong Kong Island. After signing in and leaving our luggage, we drive to Ju-long's mother, Ting, and Cheng, whom she will marry in two days. We stay for only a short while, leaving Ju-long there while the rest of us spend some time with my grandparents at Waterfall Bay Road. Ju-long will meet us at the hotel later. *The T Hotel* is a training concept hotel that provides vocational training in hospitality and tourism, and the students are attentive and friendly.

It has been quite a while since we visited the two oldest members of the family. Grandma Jiang will be 71 at the end of the year, and Grandpa Cheng turned 79 in the spring. Grandpa looks even older than the last time I saw him, and Grandma looks somewhat worn-out, probably because of her worries about her husband.

It is cramped in the small apartment, now that there are six people sharing the space. I look around; here is the same smell and warmth but, at the same time, I sense a 'disturbance in the force'. It is like a draught or drag, as if something is being sucked out of the room, but is not willing to let go.

I catch Mum's eyes. She senses it too. We look at Grandpa. It is obvious that he is not very present and his attention fades in and out. During our stay, he complains that it is cold, then hot, and over things that are trivial; some don't even make sense.

None of us speaks of the retirement home.

Before dinner, Dad takes over the kitchen, assisted by Grandma, and they finish up on what she has prepared for her family.

At dinner we talk a little about Julia, but most of the talk is about pregnancy, and babies in general. Anna directs most of her attention to Grandpa. She has told me that she feels it might be the last time she sees him. I know the feeling, because I have had it each time I have visited them for the last few years. Dad is a little here and there, being the nurturing background hum that closes in and hugs us all.

Grandpa doesn't stay up long after dinner and, for some reason, he allows Anna to tuck him in. When she comes back, I see sadness in her expression. She comes over to me sitting in Grandpa's armchair, and squeezes herself down beside me.

"It's like putting a small child to sleep. He craves attention and is not even embarrassed about it."

I give her a hug.

"It's like a human shell, where the compassion of the soul and the wisdom of his life have left him."

We look at Grandma, and she speaks to all of us.

"Thank you for not talking about the retirement home. I have tried to bring the subject up, but he strongly refuses to talk about it. 'We are doing just fine here, as we always have been,' he says.

I don't think he realizes that he is about to be a great-grandfather. It seems that he is surprised every time I mention it."

Mum brings us her view on the situation.

"He lives in the past in his mind, and has no focus on the future whatsoever. I suggest that we don't bring up the subject of moving, unless Grandpa improves and is able to contemplate the possibility."

Shortly after, we say goodnight to Grandma and are well back at the hotel, sitting in the lounge, when Ju-long returns from his visit to Ting and Chang.

"It is wonderful to see how Mother is teeming with life. She is so happy. They were both very busy, but had a hard time letting me leave. How was your evening?"

I bring him up to speed about my grandparents, and we all have a little chit-chat before we leave for our rooms. I promise to tuck-in Anna, and then we say goodnight to Mum and Dad. Tomorrow we will bring my grandparents to Repulse Bay Bach and the Tin Hau & Kwun Yum statues. I remember it being one of Grandpa's favourite places. Ju-long will accompany us, but later leave us to visit some friends.

Ju-long and I have our proper 'goodnight' and, now that I am dozing off, an uneasy feeling comes to me. It is the whole situation around Grandpa. My inner view turns dark red; the smell of plants and dirt tickles my nose. A burial? Now the chirping of birds reaches me and a light breeze touches my face. I turn my awareness to it and see the crimson dragon, Shaumbra, standing close to me in a clearing. The breeze is Shaumbra's breath that encourages me to open my 'eyes'. The place that I have come to know so well is in the land of the Sidhe, and we call it Elvendale, as I have mentioned earlier. I sense Shaumbra's inner smile and I can't stop myself smiling back.

"You're really trying to lighten my mood. You smell of mint, so you have brushed your teeth this morning!"

"Ha, I never brush my teeth and I'm always clean. It comes with a pure heart. Well… and things are different here in Elvendale than in your realm."

Shaumbra lies down and I place myself between her front legs, using them as armrests, and put the back of my head to the upper part of her chest. Hmm, I realize that I just wrote 'her' about Shaumbra. I had not thought to put a specific gender to her. I see the white dragon, Loong, as a male because he presents himself as a male Birman cat in the 3D-world. The crimson dragon, Shaumbra, could be female and I don't want to call her 'it'. She must comment on that.

"I accept the gender and see it's convenient language-wise, but please see me as a being of consciousness. Let us go back to the subject, which is your grandfather dying. People dying is a natural process, even if it was not implemented at the beginning. What is happening to your grandfather is a combination of consciousness, or the soul, slowly withdrawing its presence, and the person struggling to hold on to the human identity. When the soul's passion for both the person and the 'outer' world withdraws, there is only the ego left to interact with its pain, thoughts and emotions in reaction with the world. In the beginning, you will see only short bursts of the pure ego but, as time passes, the behaviour will be more radical. Anna recognized it as your grandfather behaving like a child."

"I now and then hear of people, just before dying, becoming quite clear and aware."

"It's the soul that is assuring the ones left behind that everything is fine. It is also the human that, at the end, relaxes and accepts the journey ahead."

"So, when a dying person chooses to let go, the process becomes much smoother and ends when the person falls asleep and doesn't wake up again."

"Yes, dying is easy; letting go might not be! I will leave you here and advise you to look at your grandfather as you used to know him, and love him as such, because it is him, not just the shell you observe these days."

When I glide back and feel my body under the sheets in the bed next to Ju-long, I still sense the hug from Shaumbra and know that I have yet another close and dear friend.

The next morning, I wake up listening to Ju-long's

slow breathing next to me. Without opening my eyes, I move under his sheets, putting my arms and legs around him. I feel happy, and the heaviness from yesterday is gone.

Tomorrow is all about the wedding, but today we have plans for making a large basket of food and drinks, like we have always done, and enjoying it in the shade at the beach; but, when we arrive at my grandparents' place, Grandma tells us that Grandpa is not well. Dad finds the perfect solution.

"We'll dine at The Lighthouse. Inside, there is a pleasant temperature and the food is excellent; I'll call them right away!"

The Lighthouse is a fish restaurant with a large, all-glass facade facing the beach, so it is an excellent choice. Dad has hired a luxurious minivan with easy access now that we need seats for seven. He could have had a car with driver from the company, but that is just not his style.

With the change in plans, Mum and Grandma are not going out shopping for their speciality foods, so we have plenty of time. Mum brings up the next idea.

"Let's do some sight-seeing around the island to work up an appetite!"

As we drive around the island, I am glad to be in Hong Kong again, even if it is just a visit. Grandpa comes to life now that he sees all the familiar places, and he starts talking about the past and is much more his old self.

As I sit in the car with Ju-long's hand in mine, I promise that, after this trip to Hong Kong, I will send an update to some of my friends: Ling in Beijing and Josephine in Shanghai, with a special hello to her grandma and the cat, Loong.

We have a lovely time at the restaurant, enjoying the food, each other's company and the view of the beach and Repulse Bay. When I think that we are about finished, we get a typical remark from Anna.

"I'm so full, but I so need a dessert… to compensate for the healthy seafood."

I feel like the big sister today.

"Go easy on the dessert, and pick a small one."

Anna has her own logic.

"Because I've had so much healthy food, I will need a gigantic dessert."

She spreads her arms wide open, and Dad grasps his glass just in time to save the contents. Now I try with plain physics.

"Anna, you had better consider your physical capacity!"

Anna replies with an assumed, grave face.

"I am really trying to live a balanced life here!"

I run out my last and, I think, very logical argument.

"But there will be a large menu tomorrow at the wedding, Anna!"

"I'm pretty sure that you can't bring today into tomorrow. Tomorrow is a quite new day… a new experience!"

Anna gets her dessert, but must give up when one third into it. Anna is Anna, and I love her for just being that!

After the meal, we drive back to let Grandpa have his nap before afternoon tea. Anna joins him in Grandma's part of the bed which, I may say, is totally understandable after her stunt at the restaurant. Ju-long is visiting his friends; probably making some arrangements for the wedding. Because Grandpa is having his nap later than usual, tea-time is postponed as well. The late dinner consists of a light soup and newly-baked bread.

The wedding day is Saturday, 15 September 2018. In the Lunar Calendar it is 6 August 2018. This gives the numbers 6, 8 and 2; all good numbers according to Chinese tradition. Ting and Cheng have chosen the *Méridien Cyberport Hotel* for the wedding party. It is part of the Cyberport amusement area next to Telegraph Bay. We have the ground level with access to the swimming pool, a podium and a garden. This floor can hold up to 330 guests.

We arrive at 4pm. Dad and I will pick up my grandparents at their home prior to the dinner at 8pm. Mum and Dad will drive them back when they feel tired. Mum has brought one of her red, handmade envelopes commonly used in China to pass on money gifts, and we have all added our share. Giving money in China isn't considered an 'easy solution'. You make the gift personal by adding a card, on which you write wishes or blessings. The card is the gift and the money covers the expenses.

There are decorations and banners in red and gold everywhere, people are busy with the last preparations, and there are quite a lot of guests already. We head for the garden and I see some young kids playing, having their parents nearby. The last time Ju-long and I were in Cyberport, we were watching a movie in one of the eight theatres in the large dome, not this hotel. We had just met again for the first time since I had moved to England. We had been very much aware of each other, and not so much of the movie.

Cheng has family, friends and business connections in Hong Kong, mainland China and all over the world, so we can expect to meet a lot of people we do not know. We can expect the arrival of the newlyweds at 5pm, and Ju-long, Anna and I meet with some of his friends and relatives to prepare some games that he and the others will arrange.

Ju-long has introduced us to the ones he knows and, now that Ting and Cheng have arrived, the garden, the area around the pool and inside the hotel are very crowded. There will be a lot of people they must greet. Ting wears an elegant, long, red dress and Cheng a crimson suit, including a waistcoat.

Oh, now you wonder how we are dressed? Properly! The invitation said the dress code is 'relaxed', probably to help the many international guests. The dress code is not about looking the best, but to show your respect for the bride and groom and to present who you are, especially if there are many guests who don't know you. Without going into too much detail, it goes like this: Ju-long wears a rose-pink suit, and I a pink, draping dress, Anna a peach dress with flower pattern and gold, Mum a yellow dress with some gold, and Dad wears a purple suit with a hint of gold. You may wonder how we got Ju-long to wear the rose-pink suit? Well, he chose it by himself! One day he came home, telling me that he had been out shopping with Julia. He goes into the bedroom with a large bag and a smile on his face.

"Just wait until you see this! I need to change."

And changed he is! I give him a warm hug.

"So cool. You even smell of wild rose!"

"Oh, it's not me, it's Julia!"

I feel Julia smiling in the wings.

Now back to the wedding. We have a wonderful afternoon meeting a lot of people and Anna, Ju-long and I spend much time with the young kids and their parents. We have made some initial connections during the games with the bride and groom, and the young adults are eager to share their experiences. My sister is much hooked on the role of being Aunt Anna, but may have forgotten that Julia is not walking around in the beginning. Ju-long also spends some time on the basketball court with some of his friends and the kids. At about 7pm, Dad and I leave to pick up Grandma and Grandpa. Grandpa looks a little tired, but is eager to attend the party. Earlier he had been a little grumpy, Grandma told me. They were both nicely dressed, Grandpa in a light-grey suit and blue tie, and Grandma in skirt and blouse with colours of sky-blue and gold.

At some point I am sitting on a stone ledge in the garden looking at a small group of trees, when I see a young woman coming towards me. She is very elegant, with her hair pinned at the top of her head, wearing a narrow dress as yellow as a dandelion and with golden sandals; her toenails are painted deep orange. She smiles.

"Hi, Mum."

"Julia!"

I recognize the expansion of consciousness and know that I am the only one who can see my daughter.

"I wanted to dress up like the rest of you, so I chose this yellow dress. I do this a lot, but I want you to see me like this. It's so beautiful."

"Indeed you are, my love. We are all so looking forward to your arrival."

"Yes, it's nice to feel welcome. You might have guessed that I'll be born without ancestral attachments and without being soaked in mass consciousness. I'll be ME."

"You've told us that indirectly, by the way you have presented yourself. Ju-long and I are giving you an initial body of our DNA and we'll raise you with your sovereignty in mind."

"As my body grows inside you, the template will shift into my own light energy body and it will be born unique to both yours and Ju-long's."

I feel for a joke.

"Light energy body; will you be glowing?"

Julia smiles.

"No, it means that the body is built of my 'personal' energy and not being as heavy as the old or normal ones. It is the same energy that I will use to express and create in my human life. Tobs calls it New Energy because it has new attributes and does not act in the old way."

"How?"

"It will not react to power and greed, and can only be activated through the I AM, the soul, me. As it is personal, it cannot be taken from me."

"Completely free of feeling any lack! How is it personal?"

"You could say that consciousness, that I AM, has burst into existence, so this energy kind of has my fingerprint on it."

"A fingerprint lock like my computer; cool!"

A thought has come to me.

"Are you an indigo child?"

Julia smiles.

"No. It's a human term for first-timers or souls with only a few incarnations, but still with connections to all the messy stuff through their parents. I'm an 'old soul', you might say but being born without karma of any kind and with a human body created entirely of my energy. I am sovereign in every way."

"No strings attached… like Pinocchio!"

"Well, Pinocchio had many other things that burdened him, which I do not have."

Then she whispers, with a smile in her eyes:

"I'll leave you now. I have a secret meeting with Gaia and some dudes, but I'm always close. Love you."

"Love you, Julia!"

I gently wipe away the tears so as not to mess up my makeup, and sit on the stone ledge for a while before going to look for the others.

I find my grandparents sitting talking with some old friends. Grandpa is very engaged in the conversation and with life shining in his eyes. Grandma looks at me and smiles. We each know what the other is thinking and feeling.

Sorry, but here I will conclude Ting and Chang's wedding. We have arranged brunch at my grandparents' the next day. After that, Ju-long and I will visit his grandparents' graves. This might give me a reason to talk to him about his dad's part of the family. Mum and Anna will take the bus in earlier, Mum to do some shopping together with Grandma, and Anna to have some time alone with Grandpa. Anna has told me that she wishes she had spent more time with Hanna and William, our grandparents on Dad's side. Now she feels, as I have done the last couple of visits, that Grandpa is near the end of his life.

Dad, Ju-long and I take it easy this morning. We only have to move some things from the wedding, now that we have the minivan. Later, we pick up Mum and Grandma at the shopping mall. As we arrive at the block where my grandparents live, Grandpa and Anna are sitting in front of the block, talking with people from around. Dad parks the van and then he, Ju-long and I stay with Grandpa while the rest go up to prepare brunch. Grandpa is in a good mood and talks a lot about the people he met at the wedding party and the subjects that had been discussed. His gestures and language are more alive as he connects to his younger days.

Having brunch feels almost as it did years back, when Anna and I were kids. In between joking, teasing, laughing and even singing, we bring everyone up-to-date. I feel that everything is right in these precious moments and that it brings harmony to the family.

Not long after finishing brunch, Anna, Mum and Dad drive to the Pok Fu Lam Reservoir and Country Park and drop Ju-long and me off by the cemetery where his mother's parents' ashes are buried, the Aberdeen Chinese Permanent Cemetery. They died about a year ago, a month apart, and I have not visited their grave. Ju-long knows where it is and he holds a ceremony. He turns to me.

"Will Julia be here?"

"She's always with you and with me, even when we are apart. Come, sit down here with me and let us invite them in. Remember that they are not in the grave – they can meet you anywhere."

His grandparents seem to want to point this out to him as well, because we fade into a circular, stone-covered terrace with three large, stone benches equally spaced in the circle. We are sitting on one of them, overlooking a lush meadow with a stream some distance away. The old people slowly arrive from the right, walking on a path. They have an age that I remember them by, but they are no longer worn out and bent over. They greet us.

"Welcome, welcome, Ju-long and Luzi. We surely get plenty of visitors these days!"

We greet them with a bow before Ju-long starts talking.

"You're looking good and seem to be fine. Other visitors?"

His grandma answers with a twinkle in her eye.

"Yes, your mother. We talked about the wedding and her husband, Cheng. I don't think she'll remember it, though. She was thinking of us during the party and we talked a while, like we are doing now. She can't take it with her into her normal state of mind, but she brought the feelings with her back. She had been in doubt of our approval of the marriage; as if we would ever judge her actions."

The old man continues when his wife has stopped, also with a twinkle in his eye.

"And there was Julia, of course!"

Both Ju-long and I are surprised.

"Oh, so early. We had hoped to tell you about her."

"She was here long before you knew of her, although we really can't talk about time around here. She has been setting up the stage for some time. I guess around the time that you, Luzi, started on your previous book last year about the Sidhe, the Elven people. She's such a dear angel!"

Grandma presents the next person.

"And your grandpa, Luzi. He has been very present lately, but I suppose you're aware of that. He looks forward to moving on."

"Yes, he has been more withdrawn for the last month or so."

Now Grandpa comes with a big surprise.

"And your father, Ju-long."

Ju-long is very surprised.

"But I thought he was mentally ill and not able to communicate. How is this possible?"

"He is withdrawn from the human world, but some of his awareness is here on our side. As Julia is stirring up some old and stuck energies, he is at a crossroads right now."

I remember what Julia had said about her being born without ancestral karma. She, and I as well, have let go of these connections. I now get a picture of a thin and tight thread that has been cut and is now whipping back to where it is attached, creating disturbance all the way down these lines. Just one cut and all can be released. Wow!

"The crossroads are still his to choose, but I guess that Ju-long has a part to play in it as well; probably his mother, Ting, too."

I hear and feel my phone ring in my pocket. I sense an uneasiness from my grandma as well.

Ju-long's grandma addresses me.

"You should take it!"

Before I am fully back in my body to the narrow focus, I fumble to get out the phone. It is Grandma.

"Grandpa has left us; he's not breathing, but looks peaceful. Could you call your mum?"

"Right away. You should call a doctor."

Ju-long has figured out the situation. We get a taxi and arrive at the same time as Anna and my parents. A car with flashing lights shows us that the doctor has arrived. We hurry up to the apartment.

Grandma is passive. Mum is with her.

"Carl will take care of it. Anna, make some tea."

We give way to the doctor, an elderly man in white coat, and Dad; shortly afterwards, the doctor declares Grandpa dead because his heart had simply stopped.

Mum turns to the doctor.

"We want to prepare him before he is taken away."

Dad makes the arrangements with the doctor, who gives us a nod before he leaves. Anna comes with the tea and Ju-long with cups. Grandpa is covered by a sheet, and Grandma lights some candles and incense.

The afternoon sun sends its beams of light into the small room, filling it with light, warmth and a feeling of peace.

A voice, out of many voices, announces in me:

"All is well!"

I look at the others and interpret what I receive.

"I sense great relief, celebration and gratitude. There is no sadness but, instead, a feeling of anticipation for a new beginning. I see large, wooden gates being slammed open and light in all colours is showing the way out of a dark room."

We all sit with tears of joy rolling down our cheeks, as we celebrate this moment with the consciousness that once appeared as my grandpa. A dear and loving soul, indeed.

We have always been open about death, dying and how we wish our bodies to be treated after our death. Cremation is the obvious choice for us. This is the fastest way to cut the bonds to the earthly plane. Others may see it as the fastest way to give the body back to Earth. Grandpa has chosen to be cremated and his ashes scattered in the Gardens of Remembrance at Cape Collinson, on the other side of the island.

While Ju-long and I leave for a walk, Mum, Grandma and Anna tend Grandpa's body. I had not expected this from Anna; she shows me yet another new facet of her person. Dad has some practical things to attend to. Mum will be the official person whose name will be on all papers. Later, he tells us that she must be the applicant who should submit, in person, the completed application form and the original copy of *"Permit to take away cremated ashes"*, at least 10 days prior to the proposed date for scattering the cremated ashes, to the Cemeteries and Crematoria office of FEHD (Food and Environmental Hygiene Department) in Hung Hom, or Happy Valley. Just that one application ensures that we will stay about two weeks in Hong Kong. She must also make a declaration that she will be responsible for any liability or related matter arising from the ashes scattering.

Ju-long, about his dad

Ju-long and I walk hand in hand down to Waterfall Bay. It is high tide, so there isn't any beach for the moment. We stand a few minutes, looking at the tiny waterfall by which I played for countless hours when I was a kid. We walk back up the concrete stairs with light-blue banister, and continue along the brick-paved path to Waterfall Bay Park. The park is just a small strip of trees, grass, a paved path, benches and playgrounds along the shoreline to one side and the Waterfall Bay Road to the other.

We start talking about my grandpa's situation, but then we move on to talk about our meeting with Ju-long's passed grandparents.

"It was nice to see my grandparents looking so well."

"They are not suffering as they did when they were alive. You must also know that they have no bodies now, but choose an appearance which you would be comfortable with. I guess they stay close to the Earth's realm to act as a reference point for the energies around you and your parents. Julia is part of this as well."

"Yes, it seems that Julia has set all this in motion."

"Ju-long, please tell me what you know about your father."

Ju-long hesitates; he has obviously not put this into spoken words very often.

"My father has, or had, a four-year-older sister and a two-year-older brother. The family mostly earned their living by harvesting the sea. They were poor and everyone had to work. Dad knew my mum from the market place; her family were farmers."

"So that was probably how they got acquainted."

"At some point, Dad found himself able to arrange with some fishermen to buy their catch. I do not know from how many boats. This way, fishermen without families could have their fish sold on the market while they were at sea. Little by little, Dad's business grew and there came a time when he could afford to marry my mother. Now they could sell both fish and produce from the farms. When I was born, they had widened the range of products and, when I was about four years old, my parents were able to get a small grocery store, not just a booth, with equipment for both fishermen and farmers."

"Where did you live?"

"We had a small apartment upstairs from the store. One morning, as Dad was down at the harbour doing some business, a fire started while Mum and I were upstairs. We were able to get out just before everything was on fire. We lost all we had and, over a short time, Dad turned more and more inside himself and, at some point, he even stopped eating. Dad was placed in a home for psychically unstable people; Mum worked here and there, always having me with her. At first we stayed with some relatives, then with her parents and, after a year or so, we got a small apartment. Later, when her parents couldn't take care of themselves, they moved in with us. Most of this my mum and grandparents have told me. I was too young to remember these things."

I help him move on with his story.

"So, when you started in school and I got to know you, you were living in the apartment with your mother. Were your grandparents there at that time?"

"No, they moved in when I was about ten years old. In the beginning, it was a huge help for Mum.

They could help with me in the morning and be there in the afternoon when I returned from school. They helped me with my homework, some cooking and cleaning, while Mum worked all the time from early in the morning to late in the evening. She had a couple of hours off during her working day and she sometimes visited our home. I usually only saw her on Saturday or Sunday, or if she came home before I went to bed."

I am shocked by his story. I knew Ting had been working a lot, but didn't know it had been so much… like in always.

Ju-long continues.

"As I grew older, I was able to help in the household. At the same time, my grandparents were of less and less use because they became too old. Later, I was able to bring some money home from my jobs, enough that Mum was able to spend more time away from work."

I know that we must use this opportunity, while Ju-long is talking openly about his past as well as his father, to make him set these family things free.

"Your mother has let go of your father. He is cut loose from that point. If you too want to totally let go of your father, I suggest that you see him in person so you can do it in a very concrete and physical way. It will help all your family. I will definitely be with you, and so will Julia!"

I witness Julia putting her etheric hands on his shoulders to fully ground him in this matter. This makes him see the situation clearly.

"In a way it will be like meeting a stranger, because I don't remember him. I have a sense, but no images first-hand in my mind. Normally, I wouldn't even consider meeting him, but I've got a different view of things."

As part of telling Ting and Cheng about Grandpa's death, Ju-long arranges a visit to their home this evening. Just him and me. Then we walk slowly from the cemetery back to my grandparents' apartment. When we are back in the apartment, Grandpa's body is ready to be picked up. I spend a few minutes with the body, knowing that it has been just a vessel for the soul. I know that our family will have a short conversation with him later, but right now his departure is too close. I imagine that it would be just after the cremation, before his ashes are scattered in the Gardens of Remembrance. Except for the close shave and the hair done, the face looks like the one I saw when he had just died. Shortly after, the body is picked up. It's placed in an aluminium casket; it will be placed in a real casket before the cremation. Dad had made the arrangements. Mum will stay overnight with Grandma while the rest of us drive back to the hotel. Tomorrow we will meet again, to discuss further details.

Ting and Cheng

Ju-long and I arrive at Ting and Cheng's place around 8pm. The apartment is part of Cheng's business area, and Ting has moved in with him to assist him in his work.

Both Ting and Cheng are there to welcome us. I smell cinnamon incense as the door opens. The immediate impression is of an apartment in the older style, much like my parents' home in England and Anna's and my childhood home here in Hong Kong. I hand Ting the flowers and toffees and we are shown into the living room. Cheng talks a lot, as he always does; about the wedding and the house, but not about their business.

I am delighted to be with them without all the wedding guests. It gives us an opportunity to be more intimate. Ju-long tells them briefly about my grandpa's death, and I say that I hope Grandma will move to the retirement home.

Cheng comments on this.

"I think it would be good for her. There are so many memories in the apartment and she will always be reminded of her husband and drawn back to a life in the past. On the other hand, it might be the same things that could make her life continue peacefully for years to come. In the end it must be her decision and her responsibility."

Ting looks at her husband.

"No matter what she chooses, we will be looking after her, right Cheng?"

"Indeed, we're family!"

"We'll all be so grateful if you could keep an eye on

Grandma."

Ting speak her mind and tells us why she doesn't feel Grandma would be a burden.

"I've lost both my parents, so it will be good to have the old lady to keep an eye on."

When Ting lost her parents, shortly after Ju-long moved to live with me in England, she became very depressed. We invited her to stay with us for a while and here she experienced a connection to the invisible creatures in and around our garden. She also encountered Loong, the white dragon with whom I work. It was a very liberating experience and she was able to open her heart and let life in. That was when she met Cheng, in a Chinese super-market in our city. I ask Ju-long to tell her about our meeting with Ting's departed parents.

After Ju-long's story, I see that Ting is uncertain how to respond, so I take over.

"As you can hear, there is a lot of clearing going on. Old connections, not useful any more, are being broken down and people are being set free to stand in their own sovereignty. I want to assist Ju-long, father to my daughter, Julia, to get his sovereignty. This will release him from his father's bonds and, maybe, set Kong free as well, maybe from his own prison. Wouldn't that be wonderful?"

I see Ting considering the situation before she gives us an answer.

"It's a good image of Kong's situation; a prison.

Kong is his own prison. If we could do something to ease his burden, I feel we should do so."

I push the conversation a little bit further.

"In the end it is Kong's choice, but we might provide the push that makes him choose."

Of course Ju-long is eager to know more about the day that changed his life.

"Mum, please tell us what happened that day with the fire."

Here I will sum up Ting's story.

First, Ting hadn't noticed the fire downstairs, because she had a small fire in the stove herself. When grey smoke came through the floor and she could hear the flames, she grabbed her child and headed for the stairs. She was blinded by smoke and she tumbled down, not sure if she would run right into the flames. She managed to get outside but first, after clearing her lungs, she could call for help. Luckily a lot of people came to help. The whole house was burning, so they concentrated their efforts on preventing the neighbouring houses from catching fire.

The next question must come from me.

"Ting, do you know where Kong lives today?"

"I can't be sure, but I think it's the Yeung Sing Memorial Long Stay Care Home. It's on Wong Chuk Hang Road, or Path, but you can check it out. It's right next to the Aberdeen Tunnel and the new Gleneagles Hong Kong Hospital."

I look at Ting.

"I don't know how we'll play this, but the main reason for the contact will be to tell Kong that he is going to be a grandfather; the second is to clear Ju-long's bonds to him, to set both of them free."

Our conversation turns to other subjects and we have a wonderful evening. It is good to see how Ting has turned into a vigorous and joyful woman, especially in contrast to how she was when she visited us last year.

Ju-long's father

The next morning Ju-long calls the care home and, after being put through to two different persons and some waiting, we have an appointment for visiting the home. This will be in the afternoon. This is also the day when Mum, Dad and Grandma will be doing some paperwork. Anna will be out on her own, visiting friends and places. Ju-long and I do not have any plans other than the visit in the afternoon.

Shortly after we arrive at Grandma's, I can tell that she has done some serious thinking and decision-making during the night.

"I knew that you all were worried about Grandpa and myself; mostly Grandpa, because of his condition. Now that you are about to be a mother you shouldn't have to worry about us. We had a long talk, Grandpa and I and, if Grandpa had not suddenly faded away that day, we would have come to the decision to move to the retirement home. It was difficult to find a time when I could reach him, especially here at the end. The situation has changed. I will be missing Grandpa in the apartment, expecting him to be here, because I now and then will forget that he has passed over. At the retirement home I'll get new friends and I know the place from visiting Ju-long's grandparents when they lived there. I want to move to the retirement home… as soon as possible."

She looks at Dad. He had told Mum, Anna and me that he had paid for an apartment since the day when the possibility was first discussed, so his answer to Grandma was not difficult.

"If we plan this right, you'll be at the retirement home before we leave Hong Kong this time. I'll make some calls to set it in motion. There will be some more paperwork to do, though."

Grandma smiles.

"You're all so very sweet. You came to attend a wedding and now see all the trouble you have to deal with."

Anna is positive, as always.

"We came for a wedding and were prepared for the possibility that you and Grandpa would be moving, so it's just Grandpa's funeral that is added."

Mum adds to the argument.

"And since we must wait at least ten days before we can scatter his ashes, we may as well take advantage of that time. I hope we'll get the date for the cremation today, or at least an estimate."

We all leave the apartment at the same time. Julong and I have decided to visit his old workplace, Pok Fu Lam Public Library, on Waterfall Bay Road. This will surely bring back some nice memories. We take the long road south through Waterfall Bay

Park, then we loop east, then north at Waterfall Bay Road to number eight.

This Saturday afternoon they will have *Storytelling for Children* in Cantonese. I see the course Ju-long used to teach: *Introduction to Library Catalogue, Internet & Electronic Resources* every Wednesday varying between adult and junior attendees. He was also assisting in the Students' Study Room.

The girl, Liling, is at the counter, like the first time I arrived in my search for Ju-long. She is very surprised to see him and she smiles.

"Ju-long! Back in Hong Kong?!"

"Yes, Luzi and I are visiting family. And guess what. I am going to be a dad!"

"Congratulations, both of you. You're living in the UK, right?"

"Yes, by the Channel, in Brighton. I'm at the university there and working at The British Library in London; especially with Chinese literature and restoration."

Liling is looking at my tummy, so I need to distract her.

"We live in a rented, 16th-century, stone house with a large garden right next to nature as well as the sea. I've just been tested positive, so it will be close to nine months before the cradle Ju-long is working on must be finished."

Ju-long smiles at Liling.

"I'm a handyman; didn't you know? We are out for a walk and I just wanted to look at my old work. It is very much the same."

We take a quick walk in the open areas before we say goodbye to Liling and walk outside. As I have the memories of Ju-long and I fresh in my mind, I pose a suggestion.

"Why don't we take an early lunch near the Wah Fu Shopping Centre? We can sit under the trees."

"A brilliant idea. I remember the first time. You picked me up in my lunch break. I was terribly nervous. You looked gorgeous!"

"And you wore the T-shirt with the two swans."

"Men in love do silly things!"

"Yes, I know. You've shown me! It really didn't matter what you wore, as long as it represented you."

We are both smiling as we walk up the hill to the café named *Howard Johnson Restaurant*.

Because we are early, it is easy to get our food and, shortly after, we take it outside to sit at a table under some trees.

We hear a lot of kids coming up the street, laughing and talking. Three young adults are supervising them. Obviously a kindergarten. Ju-long addresses the party.

"Hello there; I see you are training the grown-ups to be safe in the traffic!"

A young girl corrects him.

"We're not teaching the grown-ups, they are teaching us!"

"Oh, of course. How silly of me!"

Her friend, with whom she holds hands, decides to join the conversation.

"Next month we will have a birthday party!"

A boy next in the line joins in too.

"And we're going to visit Ocean Park!"

Ju-long shows a very surprised face.

"Both a birthday party AND Ocean Park? Nah!"

"It's true! Felicia, tell him!"

The young woman in the front explains.

"We are from the kindergarten at the other side of the shopping centre. Po Leung Kuk has its 140thanniversary this year, so we'll have a ceremony, a birthday party and the K3, the eldest kids, will have a site visit to Ocean Park."

"You're some lucky kids, that's for sure."

The first girl addresses Ju-long.

"What's your name?"

"My name is Ju-long and this is my girlfriend, Lu-cia, but we call her Luzi."

"It's an Italian name like yours, Felicia!"

"Yes, but let's move on. We'll soon have lunch."

We nod to the adults and wave to the kids as they pass by. After they have passed us and entered the centre to use a short-cut bridge on the other side directly to the kindergarten, Ju-long and I are silent for a couple of minutes. We have our parenthood and Julia on our minds.

After finishing our lunch, we walk around the area a bit until it is time to take the bus to go visiting Kong.

After arriving, we are shown into a small office to talk to a staff member who knows Kong.

The man is of normal height for a Chinese, around fifty years old with a friendly face. He wears glasses with black frames, blue shirt, dark-blue jacket and black trousers and shoes.

"Hello, my name is Mr Kwan and I am one of the staff members who work with Mr Wang. I have known him for over five years now. I will tell you a little about Mr Wang and his daily life here, since you have not been in contact with him in recent years. After that, you may decide if you want to meet him in person."

"As we have explained, me and my girlfriend, Luzi, are living in England and she is pregnant with Dad's first grandchild. We hope that this news might cause a change in his condition."

Mr Kwan points at two chairs in front of us.

"Please take a seat."

We sit down at a small, round table arranged with tea and home-made cake. Beside Mr Kwan's chair I see a large, white, paper bag with string handles.

Mr Kwan starts.

"I'll try to give you a picture of Mr Wang."

"Mr Wang is not mentally retarded and he does not take any medicine; we use psychology and personal relationships. He is gentle, withdrawn and uses no real eye-contact. He doesn't speak. I feel it's a real communication barrier. If he starts to speak, I'm sure he will appear much more open."

Ju-long has a question.

"What happens if you ask him a question?"

"Mostly he simply won't respond, or his body language will indicate his answer."

Mr Kwan continues his description of Kong.

"He is in good physical health, does simple, practical tasks and keeps his room clean, as well as his person. The home has its own professional hairdresser and Mr Wang may show up by himself, or when we suggest it is time for a haircut."

I know that one's appetite is a very good indication of one's emotional condition.

"How is his appetite?"

"He attends all meals and eats well. There is no problem there. We always have a large selection of dishes to ensure the people can get good variety and nutritious food. Food and drink are always accessible, also between meals."

Ju-long has another question.

"What about activities?"

"We have a lot of activities and Mr Wang has selected some of them. Together, we have put up a weekly plan to give a structured day, which makes him feel secure. Mr Wang attends some mild physical exercises, alone or with one other resident. He likes trips to the seashore, and boat trips if there are only very few attendees. He likes to listen to soft music and watch movies with nature and animals. He is not so much into reading."

Mr Kwan shows us a typical weekly plan for Kong. It has a nice balance between activities, meals and free time.

"Mr Wang's passionate hobby is to cut landscapes in wood or draw them on wood or paper. He cuts Mah-jongg tiles in wood and bone as well. None of his motifs contain people. It's a good hobby, because he can sit in seclusion and do his work when he needs to. We are working on making him comfortable having people around him. We can't work on improving his social skills. The problem is that he has social skills but is just not capable of using them, and that's the reason he is here. It is the opening to human contact that we are slowly, slowly introducing him to."

Mr Kwan reaches down, takes the paper bag and places it on the table.

"I want to show you some of Mr Wang's work. I, myself, am very impressed by the quality of his art-work."

First, he shows us an ink drawing made by brush on heavy paper. It is in black and grey. A mountain scene with some vegetation, a river and a waterfall.

Then there is a woodcut on a flat piece of light wood, showing two bamboo trunks with leaves. The motif is enhanced with black ink.

Now Mr Wang takes out a cloth which is wrapped around something.

"I have brought only a few of these so you can get an impression of what Mr Wang is working on right now."

They are some Mah-jongg tiles with motifs cut

in bone and then painted. The reverse is made of dark wood; every corner and edge is rounded and each side is polished. They are very beautiful. My mother makes artwork herself, so I am interested in what Kong is doing with the finished products.

"If a resident wants, he or she can sell the work in our shop or at the market. Mr Wang has agreed that, if someone buys one of his pieces, the customer must thank him in person if possible. This way, he sees the person who appreciates his work as well as the element of training for more openness."

Ju-long and I hand back the tiles to Mr Kwan and look at each other. Of course, we want to meet the man.

"We want to meet my father."

Mr Kwan gets up from his chair.

"I will go with you and introduce you. Remember, you are strangers to him. Let there be only a little talking, especially if you want any response."

We follow Mr Kwan to the wing where Kong has his apartment. Next to the door there is a plaque with a number, Kong's name and a photo almost in profile which seem to be some years old and it is difficult to see any details. Mr Kwan knocks gently on the door and waits a little while before he slowly steps into the room.

"Hello, Mr Wang. I have brought you two very nice visitors who will only stay for a moment."

We walk slowly into the room, stop about ten feet from Kong, and bow. He sits at a small table with a table light that sends a strong, white light at the tile he holds in his hand. He has his back and left side towards us, working the tile with a small knife. He does not look away from his work.

Mr Kwan continues in a casual voice, after a small pause.

"This young man is your grown-up son, Ju-long. He is 27 years old now."

Another pause.

"This is his lovely girlfriend, Luzi. They have been going to school together."

For some reason I feel that we should change focus away from us.

"We have admired your wonderful work, Mr Wang. It is truly amazing."

In the next pause we move closer and are now about three feet from the table.

Kong is not as tall as Ju-long, but has the same slender body. His hair is short and grey. He wears a light-grey shirt and a pair of dark-grey trousers. He has black, Kung Fu slippers on his feet. I address Kong.

"If I were to make a tile, I would glue the bone part and the wood part together first. This way, it's easier to hold on to it when using the tool."

I feel, more than I see, a nod from the man.

Ju-long continues.

"Luzi and I live in England and are visiting Hong Kong. Today we visit the library where I use to work. We will be staying for two weeks. We will leave you to your work now and come back tomorrow, if you allow it."

Again, a very subtle reaction that could mean anything, but a reaction nevertheless.

I bow to the man at the small table.

"Goodbye, Mr Wang. It has been a pleasure to meet you."

"Goodbye, Dad."

Mr Kwan bows.

"See you later, Mr Wang."

We walk out of the room and Mr Kwan gently closes the door before he gives his comment.

"I think it went very well. You are good at sensing the situation and changing the focus and the subject. I am not sure if you noticed the reactions. You may call me on my direct number before 8pm this evening. I hope I may see a reaction to your visit before that. Then we can plan if you should visit tomorrow."

Ju-long looks at me, sure that I have seen the faint

reactions. Then he answers.

"We noticed the reactions and I'll call this evening to hear if there is news. Thank you for your support, Mr Kwan."

I turn to Mr Kwan.

"I sensed that Mr Wang reacted positively to our short visit. I hope we can come visiting tomorrow."

Ju-long and I are shown to the front door and let out. We get to the bus stop as a bus pulls in. We are excited and talk about the meeting. I am in no doubt that we should visit him tomorrow.

As we get to Grandma's apartment, she and my parents are there and have just started on making dinner. This is nice and calming work, especially considering that Grandpa died only yesterday. Anna will not come. She will show up at the hotel later… or not.

Mum, Dad and Grandma are quite exhausted after a long day in offices talking to people, filling out forms, talking on the phone, waiting and driving from office to office in the city. A lot has been accomplished and the cremation will be on Friday, which is in four days. This means that scattering the ashes can take place at the end of next week if the Gardens of Remembrance have the time. The planning with the retirement home is in progress.

The rest of the family is delighted to hear about our

positive meeting with Ju-long's father and are full of hope for an improvement in Kong's condition.

Mum suggests that we take a day off tomorrow, which I can clearly understand.

"How about chartering a boat for a trip to Stanley Market tomorrow?"

Dad thinks it is a splendid idea.

"It will just be about five miles and the weather is good for the moment. Ju-long and Luzi can take the bus or a taxi from Stanley to visit Kong. That would be no problem."

Mum turns on her phone.

"I'll text our plan to Anna."

Shortly after, Anna replies.

"It's OK with Anna. She doesn't know when she'll be back at the hotel, but will have breakfast with us tomorrow."

We could drive the few miles to Stanley but, by combining a boat trip with a meaningful destination, it will be a more complete experience.

Tonight, Grandma wants to stay alone in the apartment. She says that she must gradually get used to being alone in her apartment, here and in the retirement home. She seems to be OK with this.

Shortly before 8pm Ju-long calls Mr Kwan at the home to hear if his dad has had some response to our visit earlier today.

When Mr Kwan had mentioned our visit later that day to Kong, Kong had looked up from his work, even if he was not looking at Mr Kwan. Mr Kwan sees this response as extremely positive, with those words, and he encourages us to come visiting at the same time tomorrow as we did today, which we agree to.

While we drive to the hotel, I doze off a bit, leaning my head against Ju-long's shoulder. Something is tickling my nose and now I find myself standing face to face with my dear friend, Loong, the white dragon with fluffy hair. He is so close that the hair on his snout touches my nose. I give him a hug and he purrs.

"There is quite a lot going on around your family these days, Luzi! But it seems that you can keep up with it."

"Julia must be responsible for a lot of it, and she is not even born yet. Synchronicity is really at work here, and she is connected to both families."

"Indeed; looking at the energy patterns, it's most beautiful; a symphony."

"The visit with Kong has given me hope that things may loosen up in Ju-long's family. Ting has started a new life and her parents seem at peace after passing over. Why is it still so difficult for Kong, even though they have been working on getting him to open up for several years?"

Loong lay down on the ground and I sit down on the ground as well, leaning up against his tummy. It's lovely to feel his slow breath working against my back. When Julia's body grows larger inside me, she must have nearly the same experience. Loom explains.

"In another life, Kong lost his whole family, wife and kids, in a fire and, for that, his wife's family punished him severely. Therefore, his reaction was so extreme in this case. Of course, it was a bad situation after the fire in this life, but nothing they couldn't have lived through. Rising from the ashes, so to speak."

I come to think of people who have an irrational response to some circumstances.

"He reacted to a different event, so to speak; a kind of automatic response to a memory in his consciousness and his DNA, a bodily remembrance."

I have missed Loong.

"We haven't spoken for a while, Loong."

"Don't be so sure about that. Your consciousness works on many levels. You have as many as 12 dream levels. You dream all the time, not only when you sleep."

"I assume that this meeting is not a dream, but an

act of consciousness."

"That is correct. We will talk about dreams another time."

I feel Ju-long's hand as he gently nudges me awake.

"Luzi, we are at the hotel."

"Bye, Loong; I love you."

Ju-long hears my last words to Loong.

"Oh, you've been talking with Loong, that fluffy beast."

"Yes, I'll tell you all about it later when we're in our room."

When I lie in Ju-long's arms in bed, I relay what Loong told me about Kong. I can see that getting an explanation is a great relief for Ju-long, as he responds:

"Now it makes more sense, don't you think?"

"Indeed. Now the reaction is in equal measure to the experience. Or one could say that the punishment must have been devastating."

It is paramount to me that the communication tomorrow with Kong should be as fertile as possible, and I ask Ju-long for help.

"Can we have a brainstorm to find some non-threatening questions, where the answer only requires a *yes* or a *no*?"

Some subjects come up.

• "Do you sell your work?" I know that we already know that he does, but the point is the dialogue.

• "Have you been on a fishing trip on the sea lately?"

• Ask him to show how he does a specific thing/task when making his things.

Meeting Kong again

It is Tuesday morning and we are starting out early to make the most of the day. Yesterday, Grandma was able to arrange a boat charter from Aberdeen to Stanley. Anna is remarkably fresh, and dressed up like a tourist… which, in a sense, she is. We have taken the chance to let the crew deliver the refreshments during the boat trip, and will find somewhere in Stanley to have our lunch. We have just picked up Grandma and are now heading for the harbour. Dad drops us off at the pier, next to the fish market, and parks the van at the Abba Shopping Centre Car Park. It can be a little tricky to find a free parking-space for the van, but I am sure he will manage.

Dad arrives about 15 minutes later.

"I really miss my Tesla X; seven seats in a normal-sized car!"

Mum pats him on the cheek and smiles.

"I'm sorry that you couldn't hire an X this time, dear. Life is so unfair!"

He hasn't lost his good mood.

"Well, what are we waiting for? Let's set sail!"

The boat has no sails, not even a mast, so it is obvious that he is joking.

Anna salutes him.

"Aye, aye, captain!"

We sail west around the small island of Ap Lei Chau that shelters the harbour from the ocean, while we have Magazine Island on the starboard side. The island had a gunpowder depot in early colonial times. The sea is calm, but we catch a little more wind as we get out into open waters. As we head south east, the fog is starting to lift and, when we are passing the peninsula, Sham Shui Kok, containing part of Ocean Park, we leave the cabin and enjoy the sun. Anna is quick with a suggestion.

"Ocean Park! We really shouldn't miss visiting it. I haven't been there for ages."

Mum sees a possibility there.

"That might very well be possible, even if we do not know when Grandma's apartment will be ready."

As if it were a cue, Dad's phone buzzes; it is the retirement home. I understand that the apartment will be available for Grandma to be moving in on Monday, next week. It seems to fit in with our time schedule. We want to pack Grandma's stuff ourselves, but we will hire a company to move it. Dad knows already the company he wants to use, so he calls them to order some cardboard boxes to be delivered tomorrow. Grandma calls the administrator of her apartment to state the date she moves out. We get Grandpa's ashes this Friday, Grandma moves on Monday and the ashes are to be released next Friday. There is time for it all, and we do not have to stress about it.

As we arrive at the ferry terminal at Stanley, we can take off our jackets and enjoy a lovely day browsing through narrow streets, and visiting shops, cafés, museums and other objects of interest.

Sometime in the afternoon, Ju-long and I take a taxi to visit Kong. The others will take the charter boat back. As we ring the doorbell, Mr Kwan comes and lets us in. He tells us that Kong is fine, and we walk straight to Kong's apartment.

Mr Kwan uses the same procedure as yesterday when we enter the apartment, including the presentation. Kong is again sitting at the table, working.

This time Ju-long and I move closer straight away, while Mr Kwan stays behind us, but still so that Kong can see him.

Ju-long says briefly what we have been doing today, emphasising the boat trip. After a small pause, he asks the first question.

"Have you been on a fishing trip on the sea lately?"

There is a pause, then Kong pulls up his shoulders. It could mean "I don't remember" or maybe the expression, 'lately' is too abstract.

Mr Kwan assists by answering the question.

"We haven't been at sea for some time. It would be a splendid idea to put in on the plan for next week. What do you say, Kong?"

Kong raises his head a little and Mr Kwan reads it as a yes.

"Great. I think Tuesday will do. I'll be at work and I can surely get a boat. I'll put it on the timetable."

He walks over to a piece of paper on the wall - it looks like a printed-out calendar - and writes in the event.

I hope I do not push our luck, and ask a question.

"I haven't been out fishing like forever. Might Julong and I have the opportunity to come along?"

Mr Kwan answers my question.

"This is entirely up to Kong. I can tell you that we do not talk much when we are fishing."

The last sentence is to assure Kong that there wouldn't be a lot of talking.

We see Kong give a slight nod, which fills me with joy. Ju-long responds.

"Thank you for giving us the opportunity to get out fishing. Luzi and I will bring some nice food for all of us if you and Mr Kwan will bring the fishing equipment."

Mr Kwan smiles.

"Surely we will. Right, Mr Wang?"

Again, a little nod. Is there a smile, too? I'm not sure. I look at Mr Kwan because I'm not sure if we can continue the conversation. He gives me a nod with his eyes.

"My mum makes different artwork too. Different kinds of pictures, many with traditional Chinese motifs, and different kinds of paperwork. Lately, she has been doing a lot of sculpting in clay, china and steel wire. She sells her things, too."

I make a pause here to clear the way for a question.

"Do you sell your things too, Mr Wang?"

Kong nods.

"That is great."

I make yet another pause before I continue.

"Sometimes I watch my mother working. This way I may learn how to do it myself. Maybe you could show me how you cut into the bone without cutting yourself?"

Kong's body language shows me that he is inviting me closer. I place myself next to him without touching him. He demonstrates his moves and then I hear his voice for the first time.

"Always away from yourself."

WOW!

"Move tool from side to side while pushing."

Wow again!

"Must be careful."

There is a pause.

"You try."

Kong hands me the tile and the small tool, which has a V-shaped cutting edge.

I carefully take the tile he puts in my hand and then the tool. I bring my hands close to my body and press my arms into my sides for maximum control. The motif is a bird sitting on a branch. It is sketched out with thin lines carefully scratched into the bone material. I pick a nearly-straight line and very carefully press the tool into the surface and push it forward, while repeatedly turning the tool a tiny bit clockwise and then anti-clockwise around its axis. I find out that the bone is quite hard to work. I'm terrified of ruining the tile, but it seems to go fine.

"Am I doing all right?"

I see his head nodding out of the corner of my eye. I explain my experience.

"The bone is hard to cut, so one must be careful that the tool doesn't slip. When I have to make a turn, I'll turn the tile, not the tool, and I'll always be cutting away from myself."

I stop the work and turn the tile in my hand.

"The cut might have to be a little deeper to hold the paint. One could make a bracelet if one only uses the bone part so it wouldn't become too thick and heavy, then drill two parallel holes sideways to add strings. That could look great if using more tiles and maybe bits between them."

Kong nods.

"Could work."

I hand him the tile and the tool.

"Thank you for letting me try. We'll leave you to your work."

Then Ju-long says goodbye.

"We look forward to the fishing trip on Tuesday."

Mr Kwan answers and shows us to the door.

"Thank you for the visit; I'll show you out."

Kong is looking at the tile in his hand. We bow to

him and leave the room. Well down the hall, I can't contain myself.

"That was crazy, wild. He talked to me!"

Ju-long is excited as well.

"More than that. He talked WITH you!"

Mr Kwan looks thoughtful.

"I'm not sure if we should wait until Tuesday before we meet again. I think we have to continue gently blowing the embers, so to speak."

Ju-long has some worries.

"The tricky part will be when I begin telling my story. At some point it will connect to the past, then to Mum, and then to her new husband."

Mr Kwan has a proposal.

"For now, you may stick to the part when you met Luzi again, moved to England, what you both are doing there and now becoming parents. Later, it might be Luzi who brings up the sensitive subjects."

Ju-long looks relieved.

"Sounds like a good plan. Can we call you tonight and check out the situation?

"Indeed, please do so. You have made me a very happy man today!"

We take the bus back to Grandma's apartment. Our plan is to have a quiet evening with her. Ju-long calls Ting and tells her about the meeting. I get an idea.

"Please ask her about Kong's favourite foods for the fishing trip on Tuesday. We must ask Mr Kwan the same."

We do not expect to be particularly hungry at dinner, so we prepare a vegetable soup with ingredients we bought at the market in Stanley.

After dinner, Ju-long calls Mr Kwan, who says that Kong has been more open in his non-verbal communication and more aware of his surroundings. Mr Kwan is very excited. The phone is on speaker.

"I have been thinking of meeting Dad when he is not working. This might bring him to be more present in a conversation. What do you think, Mr Kwan?"

Nice thinking, Ju-long!

Mr Kwan has an idea.

"The mid-morning tea in the garden may do the trick. You should be here just before 11. We will arrive from the gym, so the arousal should be high."

This becomes the plan and I am looking forward to the meeting.

The bracelet

The next morning, Wednesday, Ju-long and I stay at the hotel doing some work until we go to visit his father. The rest of the family drives to Grandma, because the boxes for her things will arrive today.

When we arrive at the home, one of Mr Kwan's colleagues picks us up at the entrance and leads us to a table in the garden. Shortly after, Kong and Mr Kwan arrive. They both look fresh, following a shower after a visit to the gym.

After the greetings, we pick up tea and bread from a serving trolley and take seats around the table.

I choose to open the conversation.

"As I live with Ju-long, I would like to tell you a little about myself. When I was 18, my younger sister, Anna, and my parents moved to England. The last time I was visiting my mother's parents here in Hong Kong, I visited them on my own. I was in the middle of writing an anthropological book about the folklore of Elves and nature spirits, and wanted to see if I could find similarities between these beings in different parts of the world. Grandma suggested that I visited Ju-long at the library where he was working. We had not had any contact since I left school and I had only had occasional contact with a few of the girls from our class. Ju-long was a great help, and it quickly became obvious that we had feelings for each other. It took me by surprise and I didn't know how to handle the situation. One day I was at the waterfall close to the altar when Quan Yen appeared to me. We met in an expanded consciousness. Another time, I met with an Elven woman, Josela, and these wonderful events have made a great change in my perception of life."

I take a short pause to give Kong a chance to absorb this unusual information.

"I tell you this because I am a few weeks pregnant, and Ju-long and I have been able to meet with the soul that will become our daughter, Julia; you are becoming a grandfather!"

Kong looks surprised, as if he is not sure if he has heard me right.

"A grandfather?"

He clearly tries to become accustomed to the fact. He realizes that life hasn't stood still, even if he might have felt that way for years. This is a tricky remark I have made, because where there is a Grandpa, there usually is a Grandma as well.

Ju-long turns the focus to Julia.

"Julia is wonderful, Dad. She really is!"

Kong stands up and we all become a little uneasy. He looks at me.

"I have something to show you."

He leads the way to his room.

From a drawer, he pulls out a piece of cloth containing something and places it on the table.

188

"Take a look at this."

He leaves it to me to unfold the cloth. Inside are some unfinished Mah-jongg tiles, but only the bone part, no wood. The tiles are smaller than the ones he showed me yesterday.

"Oh, you've been working on something new!"

Kong picks up an unfinished tile.

"I would have made you a present, a bracelet but, as you have shown me that you're skilled in this work, I would like you to work with me on this. Would you like to do so?"

He looks me straight in the eyes and, at this moment, I feel a deep connection to his soul and am deeply moved.

"Indeed I will, but I want you to draw the motifs. The pictures must come from you, Kong."

I dare to use his first name.

"From now on, I will be Luzi to you, mother to your granddaughter, Julia."

"You'll soon start to call me Grandpa because of Julia, so why not start now, Luzi?"

As much as I want to push for this opening, I am unsure if it would be too much for Kong's emotional self to handle more today.

"My grandma is moving to a retirement home, so

Ju-long and I must help her pack. Would it be OK if we start working on the bracelet tomorrow?"

I hope he is not disappointed.

Ju-long comes up with a brilliant suggestion.

"Dad, then you can prepare some pictures so they will be ready by tomorrow."

Perfect, my sweet Ju-long.

"Oh, I see. That would be perfect, wouldn't it?"

I agree with him, to reinforce the idea of starting tomorrow.

"It would be absolutely perfect."

There is a pause, because I want the timing of my next comment to be perfect.

"Grandpa, in my family, as I'm half English, we are hugging… well, a lot. May I give you a hug as we leave?"

Kong spread his arms and I give him a gentle hug. There is no awkwardness in his hug; it feels natural.

"See you tomorrow, Grandpa."

I hope Ju-long will use this chance as well. He walks towards his dad.

"As I'm part of Luzi's family now, I'm used to getting and giving a lot of hugs!"

They hug for some time, and I hear Julia laughing in joy, being the lead voice in a large choir.

As they let go, Mr Kwan suggests that they both see us out. He has tears rolling down his cheeks, but quickly removes them before we reach the reception desk.

As we walk to the front entrance, I take Kong's hand.

"This Sunday I lost my grandpa, my mother's dad. Today I kind of got a new one, at least one for Julia."

"It feels good to be a grandpa. See you both tomorrow afternoon."

Ju-long and I take a taxi to Grandma's apartment.

We are speechless and sit silently for a while, contemplating the visit. Then Ju-long breaks the silence.

"Dad took us totally by surprise."

"He seems to have been quite surprised himself."

"What will I be doing tomorrow while you are working on the bracelet?"

"You could tell him about your life, starting shortly before we met again. Remember, the work with the tiles is to calm both thoughts and feelings, because it takes focus. Tell just a little at a time. When I become part of the story, I'll add to it.

"And about Mum and Cheng?"

"Well, I could take that part, starting with Ting meeting Loong in our garden at our home. I was there too, when she and Cheng met in the store."

Ju-long calls his mum to tell her what we have experienced today. Soon after, we are at Grandma's block. As we enter the apartment, I can't help myself, but shout while taking off my jacket and shoes.

"Julia has got a new grandpa!"

Mum shows up in the hall, her face being a big question mark.

"What?"

"We have been talking with Kong and, tomorrow, he and I will make a bracelet of Mah-jongg tiles for me."

"You've really got him to open up!"

"I think it's the situation of becoming a grandpa. I'll give Julia the credit."

"And I've got my dad back, even we haven't talked that much."

"When will you be there tomorrow?"

"In the afternoon."

As we walk into the small living-room, I see they have been packing some of Grandma's things into boxes. Dad is assembling a box and Grandma is sitting in what used to be Grandpa's armchair. She smiles.

"It's so good to hear that Mr Wang is back."

I can't see my sister.

"Where is Anna?"

Dad stretches his back.

"She's out somewhere. There isn't really space for so many people when we are packing."

I have another question.

"What about the ashes on Friday?"

"They will be given to the Gardens of Remembrance. They receive ashes from the crematoria all the time, so it will be delivered before next Friday, when we will scatter the ashes."

Ju-long has been looking around the apartment.

"I'm sure we can get everything in boxes in a relatively short time. Maybe we could use a day of the weekend in Ocean Park, maybe Sunday, so Grandma Jiang won't have to be in the apartment filled with boxes."

Dad lights up.

"What a splendid idea. I think we can all agree to that. I'll check it with Anna right away!"

Ju-long keeps going with organizing.

"Luzi, how about you and I help Grandma with packing tomorrow morning?"

"Yes, let's do that; we can still visit your dad in the afternoon."

While we are preparing to move Grandma's things on Monday, she is having her meals with us in different places in the city. She prefers to sleep in the apartment, though.

Kong's dream

This Thursday morning Ju-long and I spend together with Grandma, helping her pack. Mum and Dad pick us up for lunch; Anna is out somewhere. In the afternoon we visit Kong. It plays out much like the day before.

Mr Kwan picks us up at the reception desk and introduces us to Kong. We slowly approach the table and Kong shows us two tiles on which he has drawn and then scratched the image to prepare for the cutting tool. It's easier to use the cutter when you have a groove to follow.

I pick up the cutter and very carefully start to cut the first motif. In the beginning Kong keeps an eye on me, but then he concentrates on a new sketch. At first we work in silence, but then I turn to Ju-long.

"Ju-long, why not tell your dad about yourself?"

Ju-long says a little about his childhood and school,

and I add a few comments to the things I have been a part of as well. Mr Kwan says that he must make a small errand, but will be back soon. He is gone only a few minutes and, when he returns, he sits in the only armchair in the room.

At some point a young man shows up with tea and biscuits, and we have a short break while pouring the tea and eating a biscuit.

Later, Ju-long talks about his adult life and his different jobs, including the general work and teaching at the library.

I hand Kong the first tile and he holds it close to his eyes, turning it in the light.

"When you want to make a broader line, you simply cut deeper. The triangle edge of the cutter will then widen the groove."

"Yes, of course. That's why you in some places have made three lines, the centre and the edges on each side. Let me have the tile again."

We work a little longer, until Mr Kwan suggests that we stop for the day. There is only a very little to clean up, and Ju-long and I are quickly done and ready to say goodbye. I turn to Kong.

"I feel that I've been more confident with the cutting procedure. It's only a matter of practice. I thank you for the opportunity to learn this skill, Kong."

We bow to Kong and Mr Kwan shows us out.

As we sit in the taxi, I take Ju-long's hand and look him in the eyes.

"Tomorrow will be the day when we must mention Ting and Cheng. I'm sure that Julia would not have started Kong's opening if she weren't pretty sure that it would succeed."

Ju-long shows me a little, nervous smile.

"Yes, tomorrow will be the big day!"

"Don't worry. Everything will be fine."

I sense into the situation and there is something I can't quite put into words.

"I think we are in for a surprise, dear."

I will move forward to Friday afternoon, when Ju-long and I are visiting Kong again to work on the bracelet project.

Mr Kwan comes to the reception desk to pick us up.

"I have been waiting for five years for Mr Wang to open up, and now it happens almost in an instant!"

His comment makes me put the way I see the situation into words.

"In the beginning, Mr Wang had shut down to withdraw from what he saw as an irreversible, catastrophic incident. Later, when there was some

196

distance to it all, he had no reason strong enough to engage in the world again, so his closed-down situation continued. I see Julia being that reason for him, much more than his son and his girlfriend showing up. Sorry, Ju-long. Ju-long draws strings to the past, while Julia is the new life that points to the future."

"It's OK, Luzi. I think you're right. This is exactly the right moment to bring Dad back to the world, even if I don't know what that means in practical terms."

As we enter Kong's room, after Mr Kwan has knocked on the door frame, Kong approaches us with a smile.

"Greetings, Ju-long and Luzi. I have the first three tiles ready, but first I'll tell you about a dream I had last night."

Ju-long and I take a seat at the small table opposite Kong. Mr Kwan leaves us, with an excuse that he has forgotten to sign some papers.

"Yesterday I became very sleepy after you left; I even had to take a nap at some point and go to bed shortly after dinner."

Kong starts his story.

"I am in a dark tunnel. I hear someone call my name. It sounds hollow in the tunnel. I am a little frightened. I hear the call again.

'Kong!'

"I walk in the direction of the voice. After a short walk, I realize that I'm in a misty forest and I can now see tree trunks close to me but, when I look up, it is still dark. I smell the dirt, and the ground is soft to walk upon.

'Kong!'

"It is a woman's voice. I see a faint light in the direction in which I am walking. As I slowly move forward, I get the feeling that I am walking in a forest early in the morning, approaching the rising sun.

'Kong!'

"Now the fog seems to slowly withdraw from the path and the light increases its intensity. The path now widens and there is more space between the trees. I look up and can now see the lower branches. As I move forward, a narrow, wooden bridge appears. I can hear water running under it.

'Kong!'

"I am no longer afraid, and increase my pace while crossing the bridge. As I reach the highest point of the bridge, the fog blows away and I see a large clearing with grass. The sun has just passed the treetops in the far distance on its way up. Further away there is a large, white rock and a shape is standing next to it.

'Kong, over here!'

"The call is from the woman. She is resting one arm

198

on the rock. I feel a great urge to meet her and now I am almost running over the lush covering of grass. I look down; it is wet and there are a lot of flowers which are closed, waiting for the first beams of the sun to wake them. I look up again, focusing on the woman. I now see that she is wearing a long, golden dress with golden-red ornamentation. I feel that I know her somehow.

'Grandpa, it's me, Julia!'

'Julia?'

'Give me a hug. In my family, we are hugging… well, a-lot.'

"I remembered your words from your visit, Luzi.

"As we hug, I am surrounded by a beautiful smell of wild roses and a feeling of great love and peace.

"When we withdraw, I look into two clear, green-blue eyes and, for some reason, I feel it is the Virgin Mary. I hear her wonderful laughter.

"'There may be a hint of another Mary, Mary Magdalene, but that's not important. I am ME!'

"I don't know what to say. I stand there, staring at her beautiful face flanked by long, brown hair with a golden tiara with gems in the same colours as her eyes. She smiles.

"'It took you some time! I feel that I've been calling for you for ages. We couldn't meet until you were ready. Now, I want you to meet one of my dear friends. It's the dragon, Loong.'

"She points to the white rock with her hand. I see it is not a stone, but fur, white fur. Slowly the fur rises up at the end closest to us, and the head of a dragon emerges.

"'I call myself Loong. I am a good friend of Julia's parents and now we are friends too, Kong. Interesting, Kong Wang! Your name means Sky King in your language. This name suits your primary colours: blue and white.'

"What does one say the first time one stands face to face with a dragon, not a fierce one, I may add?

"'May I touch you?'

"I feel silly after asking that question.

"'Only if you promise to rub my belly!'

"He is laughing as loud as thunder, and I must laugh myself. Julia helps me out.

"'Loong gets that question a lot and he loves being so irresistible. Roll over and show us where it itches!'

"Loong rolls over onto his side and shows his furry belly. Julia leads the way and, shortly after, the dragon is purring like a gigantic cat. I haven't felt so joyful for a long, long time, which I tell them.

"'Then take this joy with you as you leave this place. Our message to you is that all is well and things are usually much more different than they seem and feel.'

"Then I woke up, still with the smell of wild roses in my nose and the sense of long, fluffy hair in my hands. Then I knew that all is well, as Julia said."

We are all in tears and Kong is suddenly laughing.

"I haven't spoken so many words in the last twenty years in total! I have made a sketch of Julia and Loong, but I don't want you to see it before it's finished."

"That's fair enough, Dad. We look forward to it."

I feel I must make a statement that will be crucial later today.

"Kong, I hope you got the point that when Julia said that all is well, it means that nothing is wrong."

Kong nods and tells us what he thinks.

"Since nothing is wrong, everything must be all right, even if it might seem wrong."

I want to give Kong a little more information and, at the same time, show him that we know what he is talking about.

"From your description of the place in your dream, I guess that it is a place in a world we call Elvendale. It's not in a dream, but another consciousness, or what you might call another dimension. One day you'll see Elvendale City and meet some of the people there, especially Josela, who is the first one I met in Elvendale. Well, let's get to work."

Ju-long pulls up a chair for himself.

"While you're working on the tiles, I can tell you a little more about my life and how Luzi changed everything."

Kong opens the cloth with the small tiles.

"I have only three tiles with sketches ready, because I've spent some time with the sketch of Julia and Loong. As you work on the first three, Luzi, I'll draw the next one and then mark it up with a pricker; you might call it an awl."

As I sit at the table working with the first tile, '1 Bamboo', a bird, I feel that we have been here for hours. I have been so immersed in Kong's story that I have experienced it myself, not just as if I were there. That is the great thing about consciousness, it doesn't require time.

Ju-long continues his story from yesterday and talks about his mother and her job at the mall, about her parents moving into their small apartment, and about her breakdown as she loses them both within a month. Then he tells how she stays with Ju-long and me in England for a month to recover from the emotional shock.

Here I take over and tell Kong about Ting sensing the nature spirits and Loong in our lush garden, and how this event managed to open her up to the joy in life. Here I must mention the divorce between him and Ting, not knowing if he is aware of this fact or not. I also say that his part of the family has cut off any connection with Ting and Ju-long. Kong does not react to this, so I must conclude that he accepts this as a fact.

I continue with the special story of how Ting met the salesperson, Mr Cheng Fan from Hong Kong, in the mall and how naturally they communicated. I end my story with their marriage and the death of Grandpa.

"To me, all these things lead up to a clearing of families and into the emergence of Julia as the turning point of the two families, Wang/Yu and Guan/Cane."

Kong opens to a great insight.

"Things do not happen in a vacuum, they are tied together. I imagine a large dance floor where people are participating in a common dance."

Ju-long adds some strokes to this painting.

"At the same time, each dancer is free to choose how to dance, but still recognising the other dancers."

Mr Kwan is the tea lady today, as he comes through the door with the serving trolley. There are four cups, so it seems that he has some time to spend with us.

"It is becoming a little crowded in here. Please take

what you want and I'll place the trolley outside the door."

Kong shows that he is opening-up to the outer world.

"Next time, we'll be working in the workshop because there is more space, if that's all right?"

Kong looks at Mr Kwan, who then looks at me with surprise and a silent question. I answer.

"I'm sure we wouldn't take up much space in the workshop, and I'd very much like to see it."

Mr Kwan agrees.

"Sure, that's no problem. When you know what time you're coming, I'll put you on the timetable."

We spend the rest of the afternoon with the tiles, and Ju-long gets the job of polishing the raw tiles after he and Kong have cut them out to the right size from a larger piece of cattle-bone.

Now it is Friday evening. Today, Grandpa's body was cremated so, in that respect, it will not anchor him in this world. Before we go out for lunch, we gather at the apartment to connect with Grandpa. He is instantly present and he speaks to me, but not in words. This doesn't take any time, so I can relay the conversation directly to the others.

"As you know, I'm playing the role of your grandpa, Cheng, but I'm not that person, I am ME."

He smiles and continues telling me about his human character. He has the same first name as Ting's new husband.

"Cheng was worried that he might pass away shortly after his wife and he had moved to the retirement home, like Ju-long's grandparents did. On the other hand, it would take away the burden that his wife would face if he died before her and, even more, if she died before him, which might happen even though he was weaker than her."

Now Cheng's soul talks from its own focus.

"Because a lot of clearing up is taking place in the families, it would make little sense to postpone his death and my disconnection beyond the message of Julia's arrival. It's like the dance that Kong talked about the other day. As you could see, Cheng had a really good time at the wedding and we can say that he tied the last knots in his life and said goodbye to all of you in his own way."

I sense that the conclusion is coming up.

"Cheng's human essence is no longer present, and the spreading of his ashes will be a more practical act of returning his remains to the Earth in gratitude. When you think of Cheng, think of the time you had with him in the past, rather than questioning if he is all right where he is. The wisdom which will derive from his life will be a part of me, so all is well. Blessings from ME."

Grandma is the first to comment.

"Thanks. An unsentimental message that states that there is no need for grieving. Each human life has its time and the wisdom of that life is eternal."

I add my own experience from the meeting.

"I felt gratitude from this soul to life itself, for the wisdom and the joy of experiencing. This means that it's not the experiences that are wisdom, but the joy of experiencing the experiences. Do you see the difference?"

Anna clears up something for herself.

"So, what we judge as good or bad is purely a human thing. At that point there is no judgement whatsoever from the soul. In the eye of the soul, the human can't do anything wrong."

I want to show that the opposite is equally true.

"The human can't do anything right, either. The soul is not capable of judging. There are rules, morals and ethics in the human world, but spirit, from which the soul springs, can't judge."

Mum looks at me, a little questioning.

"The word 'springs' is not a word you would usually use."

"When I connect like this, one can say that I connect to a larger part of me. The part that turns my experiences into wisdom. My master self, that has seen all my souls' lives."

I am surprised about that answer. I do not know the term 'master self'. I get a response from an inner knowingness.

"You might not know the term, but I, the master self, you've always known. If I'm not there every moment of your life, how can I distil your life's wisdom?"

"And I, the I AM, have always been with you. If I'm not there every moment of your life, how can I enjoy these moments?"

I start to cry because I am so overwhelmed by this compassion that washes over me. The others are looking at me, so I must respond.

"All is well, let's have some lunch."

Ju-long puts his arm around my shoulders and we walk down to the van. I'm silent during the drive to the restaurant. I smile at Ju-long to assure him that I'm fine. I contemplate the information. We are a trinity, not the Father, the Son and the Holy Spirit, but the I AM, the Master and the human.

I see the circumpunct, a dot in the middle of a circle. The dot is the I AM, the space is the Master and the edge, the ring, is the human, living.

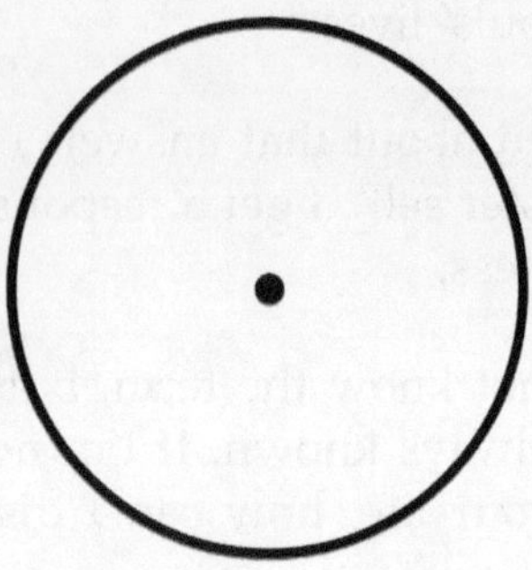

Now the circumpunct tilts a little and becomes an ellipse. It becomes a 3-dimensional figure and I see that the edge is a spiral which represents all human lives.

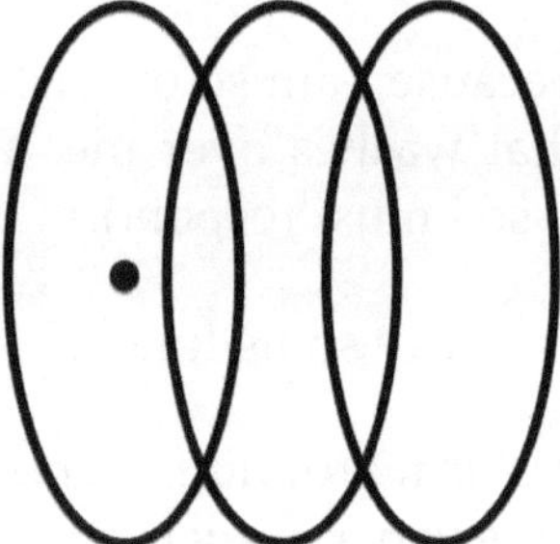

The figure turns back to become a circle with a dot in the middle, but now a curved line or spiral appears from the circle to the dot.

"This is a crude picture to illustrate this trinity."

"You've been told that this life has been chosen to gather all lives and its aspects and integrate them into this one. This 'integration' is symbolized by the spiral going from the outer circle into the centre and it is this life allowing all lives and aspects in. It's drawn as a spiral to illustrate movement or dynamics. This special spiral touches the outer life spiral of all lives, moving through the wisdom and touching the I AM."

"You are us because we're not separate. We are a common consciousness with three facets."

At the restaurant I feel spaced out, still having the close connection to the trinity. I tell the others that I have had a very personal experience and that they should not expect further details, but I am fine.

It is Saturday morning and I have had a refreshing night's sleep. Better than I have had in a long time. Today, Ju-long and I will visit Kong in the afternoon and it is from here I will continue my story.

We are together with Kong in the workshop, continuing our work with the tiles for the bracelet, and he shares some thoughts he has had about how it should look.

"First, I had the idea of separating the tiles with small dice but, later, I felt that they would be in the way of the expression, so to speak. Let's find out how many tiles we need."

Each tile is a little more than half an inch in width, so we calculate that we must make fifteen of them. Kong has already made a white dragon, very apropos his meeting with Loong, and I suggest the red and the green dragons as well. The traditional four flowers are made as four women. He has finished painting one of them in a golden and yellow dress, which I presume must be Julia from his meeting with her. We agree on the rest to be the four winds, 1 circle, 1 bamboo (the bird) and two of the numbers. Some of them are already in the making. The bracelet will be assembled with black elastic.

I must tell Kong about our plan for the rest of our stay in Hong Kong.

"This will be the last visit before our fishing trip. Tomorrow we'll be visiting Ocean Park, as we've done years back. On Monday, my grandma is moving to the retirement home and, on Friday, we'll be spreading my grandpa's ashes in the Gardens of Remembrance. Next Sunday we'll return to England."

Ju-long and I have agreed that I should ask Kong about his family, because I have no attachment to them.

"Kong, do you have any contact with your parents and siblings?"

"No; for some reason which I no longer remember, we never communicate. To be honest, I don't feel any bonds to them. I do not know where they live, or even if they still live. I would like to meet your family, Luzi. Your parents, sister and your grandma. I feel more of a connection in that direction."

"I'm sure we can do it after the fishing trip. Except for spreading the ashes, we have some days free before we leave. How do you feel about meeting Ting?"

"I have thought of that, but I'm unsure about it and, of course, if Ting wants to meet me at all; and her new husband."

"I feel that, if we could in time mend the tie between you and Ting, maybe with Julia being the thread, it will bring much balance to the family. Now we ARE family, due to Ju-long. As for Ting's new husband, Cheng, I think he'll let you in as well. Don't you think so, Ju-long?"

"I see Cheng as a man with a big heart and an open mind, who takes people as they are. He knows you're my father and Ting's former husband, but he will meet you as the person you are; he can't meet you as the person you once were. Especially as he didn't know you back then."

I make a suggestion.

"Maybe a meeting on neutral ground would be the most beneficial. In nature actually!"

Ju-long is sincere when he turns to his father.

"Dad, there really are no enemies. No one wants to hurt you or blame you."

"I know, I know, Ju-long. It's just these human

emotions that are in the mind and the body. One can't just kick them out."

I try to make Kong see things differently.

"That might be true, but you can choose how you react when they show up. So long as you're the master in your house, so to speak, the one who's in charge, you'll be all right."

Ju-long gives him yet another different way to look at those things.

"You may see them as noise, as children playing outside your house, but nothing you have to react to."

Kong lights up.

"That's a great picture of the issue, Ju-long."

Ju-long smiles.

"I guess it was Julia who slipped that comment in! She's most present right now."

Now the focus is on Julia and the future, and we continue our conversation as well as the work with the tiles. Ju-long and I will visit Ting and Cheng to talk about a meeting with Kong when we leave him today. Ju-long calls his mother and we are now invited for dinner. I call Mum to tell her that we won't be joining them for dinner tonight. The rest I must wait until tomorrow to tell.

When we leave Kong, all the tiles have been polished and carved, and have holes for the elastic. Now Kong can use the days to come to paint the remaining ones and assemble the bracelet. So much love has been put into this particular piece and I look forward to wearing it.

At our visit to Ting and Cheng, they are surprised that Kong now is so open that he even requests a meeting. They are both positive in having a meeting and we talk about where the meeting could take place. We end up with Deep Water Bay Beach, which is only four minutes' drive from Kong's home. Ju-long consults with Mr Kwan, who suggests Wednesday afternoon around 3pm, the day after the fishing trip. He will talk with Kong about it and return with an answer sometime tomorrow.

The next day, Sunday, while we are having breakfast at the hotel, Mr Kwan calls Ju-long to tell him that Kong is pleased with the meeting arrangement this Wednesday. He had insisted on calling us right now, even though Mr Kwan had suggested waiting until later in the day.

After breakfast, we pick up Grandma and drive to Ocean Park.

The park has grown since my last visit, but I feel less drawn to the attractions. Anna is disappointed as well, partly because she had higher expectations and partly because her memory of the feelings she had in earlier experiences will not equal today's feelings.

"This is really not as much fun as I remember it!"

I give Anna my explanation for this very common phenomenon.

"When we were here as kids and young, we experienced everything without comparing it to anything, and we were excited about it. Now we are boring adults, expecting the same kick or rush from hormones that were much more potent in our systems when we were young. I think it might be different if we were actually here with some kids who really enjoy the visit."

"I just have to wait for Julia, then!"

Grandma laughs at Anna's impatience.

"Then you might have to wait a couple of years. Children must have a certain physical maturity to meet your expectations, Anna."

Dad, who is always quick to find a solution, offers his help.

"I suppose you could borrow some kids of the right age. Their parents may even pay you for the time you relieve them… both kids and parents."

Ju-long teases her.

"You were quite loud at the Raging River, so you must have enjoyed it to some degree."

"Well, yes. Except the water cannons. They were too much."

Mum has her say as well.

"I saw you enjoying the water cannons when you were firing one yourself, but I guess that's a different story!"

The attractions may not amuse us to the same degree as in the past, but I'm sure that we enjoy each other's company more. Personally, I enjoy the animals most, especially at the Ocean Theatre with sea lions and dolphins.

Anna suddenly shouts out.

"Wow! Julia said that we can play anytime, and then she took me out for a ride on Loong. That was awesome!"

I smile. I have experienced that myself. It was when Josela and Loong showed me Elvendale City for the first time.

We have an early dinner in the park before we drive to Grandma's apartment. Tomorrow morning we will move her things to the retirement home, so we have this last check. Ju-long and Dad disassemble the last pieces of furniture. Only the few things Grandma needs for making breakfast are left out.

This night I wake up and ponder Grandpa's behaviour in the months before he died. Julia responds to this.

"If a person is NOT CONNECTED to the I AM and

the Master Wisdom, it would be solely egotistic, but they would still have the instincts to take care of their young. The I AM provides the joy, and the Master the compassion. The human mind can only produce emotions which are neuro-chemical reactions to its judgement. A person can learn some behavioural skills that look like compassion, but it is only for personal gain, even if it does not recognize it. Love is the mind's imitation of true compassion, and happiness is the mind's imitation of joy. To the person, these emotions are real. Again, this is only if the person has not allowed any connection with the soul and the wisdom. There can be different degrees of connection. I'm sure you have experienced such people."

The fishing trip

It is Monday morning and we are having an early breakfast. A little later, when we arrive at Grandma's apartment, she has packed the rest and is ready for the removers to pick up her stuff. We have used the removers before and they are right on time. Grandma does not want a company to clean the apartment so we form two teams, a cleaning team in the old apartment and an unpacking team in the new one. The new apartment is made especially for elderly people and is suitable for a wheelchair, which demands more space and wider doors. Ju-long and I are the cleaning team and spend the first hour outside the block, sitting under the trees and talking about how things seem to fall into place.

During the day, Ting and Cheng visit us for a short time in the retirement home. They have agreed to keep an eye on Grandma when we have gone back to England, so they come to make the connection. Grandma has been visiting some of her friends at the home, some of whom she knows from her connection to Ju-long's mother's parents before they died. They make her feel welcome, as does the staff.

At the end of the day, Grandma has the new apartment ready for moving in. She might shift around some things but, all in all, she has a new home. Some of the elders have been out shopping, so Grandma will be cooking and dining with them tonight.

Apropos the night, we have been busy all day and I am looking forward to getting to bed. Shortly after dining at the hotel, Ju-long and I snuggle in bed, enjoying each other before saying goodnight.

Ju-long and I are up early for shopping to prepare the food basket for our fishing trip with Kong and Mr Kwan. As *The T Hotel* is a training hotel, Dad has talked them into allowing Ju-long and I to use a small corner in the kitchen area for our purpose. At 11am, the boat will leave from Aberdeen Harbour and we want to be there well in time.

We step out of the taxi at ten to eleven and get two large baskets from the boot. The boat charter delivers the drink. The small boat has a captain and a sailor, and the sailor who, to my positive surprise, is a girl, helps us with the heavy baskets. Kong and Mr Kwan have arrived just before us and are busy putting on their lifejackets. When they have finished, we say our hellos and put on our own jackets. Today, Mr Kwan is the host, representing the home where Kong lives, and he tells the captain that we are ready. Now he turns to us.

"A wonderful day for our small fishing-trip. The fog has lifted and the wind and the sea are calm. The wind will increase when we get further out, but I see you have your jackets with you. As you know, it's a 5-hour trip. We will head about ten miles out south-southeast to get into the sea current between the inner islands and outer ones."

Ju-long has been looking around.

"I see that there is plenty of fishing gear!"

"Yes, the boat charter takes care of this. We use them often and their things are in good shape; as is the boat."

I start a conversation with Kong.

"Kong, how is the bracelet coming along?"

"It's finished, but you will have to wait until we are back at the harbour; I won't risk anything here out at sea."

"Sure, I can understand that, but still I'm very excited about the result. Another question; what are we using for bait?"

"It's in the white bucket with a lid over there. It's squid meat."

I walk up to the captain at the wheel and he shows me his electronic map system and the radar. Our course is set to the centre of the largest of the three other islands, Dangan Dao.

"We'll stop the engine when we're clear of Po Toi."

He draws an imaginary line from the island Po Toi parallel to Dangan Dao and puts his finger on the course line shown on the map.

"Around here. We're usually lucky to reel in some catch in these waters."

"What kind of fish might we catch here?"

"Mackerel and the fish that prey on them, ma-hi-mahi, tuna and maybe even barracuda."

I nod and turn around. From here I see that Ju-long, Kong and Mr Kwan are talking; probably about fishing by the way Mr Kwan moves his arms to show the size of a fish. I walk back to them and, shortly after, the captain stops the engine and signals the sailor to drop the anchor.

Kong opens the bucket, with bait already cut into suitable pieces and, shortly after, the hooks with bait are thrown in four different directions into the sea. The sailor stands close by to see if we need assistance but, after a while, she goes below to make some tea.

Ju-long sighs.

"What a lovely silence now that the engine has

been turned off!"

I tell him about our common work.

"Kong has finished the bracelet; the paint is dry and all. I'll get it when we are back on shore. I'm so looking forward to seeing the result."

Kong tells me that it is best to fish at night, when it is dark. I create my own theory about that.

"Fish use a lot of time and energy looking out for predators that they can spot from some distance. When it is dark they cannot see very far and, when there is no danger in the immediate vicinity, they feel safe and use their attention to find food. One might say that they are stupid but, on the other hand, why fear something that might not be there?"

Kong responds to this.

"The theory is not bad, Luzi! They have a larger room to check for predators during the day and only a closet at night."

Ju-long adds his comment as well.

"The mackerel move in shoals, so there are many eyes to look for danger. It might not be so relevant to them."

I get another idea about fish in shoals.

"Or, many fish make more commotion and draw

more attention, no matter whether it's day or night."

Kong gives a cry. He's the first to get something on the hook.

"It might be a mackerel. It doesn't put up that much of a fight."

I can see the silvery silhouette of the fish as it is pulled through the water towards the boat. When it breaks the surface, it is indeed shown to be a mackerel, with the beautiful, metallic skin looking like a sword blade made from many layers of steel. Kong pulls out the hook with a fast twist of the wrist, kills the fish with a stab in the neck with a knife, and throws it in a large, plastic tub.

"Our first catch!"

The fish makes me think of dishes.

"I love cooked mackerel, boiled, with salt and herbs and served with rice and sauce."

Kong smiles. In this moment he is happy. I see the same smile on Ju-long's face.

Kong fits a new piece of bait to the hook and throws it out again. Now the fishing begins and we all pull shiny fish out of the water. Shortly after my bait is in the water, a new fish bites and I start to reel it towards me. Suddenly, the fishing-pole is nearly pulled out of my hands.

"A shark. I've caught a shark!"

Kong brings his knowledge up.

"It might be a mahi-mahi. They prey on mackerel and they are tough to get inside the boat."

I and whatever is at the other end have a long and hard struggle. Shortly before the fish breaks the surface, Kong shouts.

"It's a mahi-mahi; and a fine one."

He grabs it with a boathook, because the fish becomes heavy when it is lifted out of the water.

"I thought it would be bigger… with all that fighting."

Kong kills it with the knife and puts it in the tub.

Ju-long has taken pictures of me and Kong, and now he wants us to pose for him.

"This is the first photo of my dad and the mother to my daughter."

I can see that he is moved.

I change the subject.

"If you can find the time, gentlemen. Let's wash up and get some lunch."

The sailor has arranged the table with everything one could think of. I look closely one more time. Where had all that food come from?

The sailor smiles.

"I couldn't get it all on the table, so you'll have to take the rest from the small table mounted at the bulkhead."

Ju-long smiles and turns his eyes upwards.

"I told you there was enough… even with one basket!"

I laugh.

"We should have brought Anna!"

We enjoy the meal and each other's company, including Kong. There is some casual talking, but not a lot. As we are close to finishing our meal, I dare to ask Kong about the morning when their house burned down. I feel that here, out at sea, could be an opportune moment.

"Kong, can you remember what happened when you lost the house?"

"I've thought a lot about it lately and I feel it would be good for me to get it out, and necessary for Ju-long to know the truth seen from my perspective."

I hold his hand as Kong tells the story. I do not know if he realizes it.

"One morning I was walking home from the harbour after doing business with some fishermen. I saw Ting, with my son in her arms, coming running towards me. She was shouting something and she looked very dirty. When she came closer, I could hear that she was shouting that the store was on fire and that they had almost been caught in the flames. I made sure that they both were OK and then we ran back to the store. A lot of people were busy putting out the fire, and emptying the houses nearby in case the fire would spread.

"Our house burned to the ground, including all our belongings, and some of the neighbouring houses had taken some damage but weren't burned down. We were left with nothing and I had some debts here and there, which is only natural when you buy and sell, but I had no way of paying it back. Worst of all, I felt that I was not able to take care of my wife and child.

"The fire had started downstairs, where I had made tea and breakfast before I went to the harbour early in the morning, while Ting and Ju-long were still asleep upstairs.

"At first, I blamed Ting for not having been careful with the fire, but she was sure that she had only used the fireplace upstairs to make food for our son and herself. Then I blamed myself for all sorts of things; I needed to find a specific thing to blame for this devastating accident.

"Our families wanted to help, well knowing that they had very little themselves, but I was proud and wanted to take care of my family myself."

After a short pause to let the story sink in, I ask Kong if he would join me on a conscious journey to Elvendale.

"Yes, I would, very much so. Everything is so calm and gentle there."

I guide him to the front deck and up to the stern, where we can sit looking out at the ocean with our backs to the cabin windows. I have Kong on my left side.

"Take my hand, close your eyes and focus on the smells you receive."

I know where we end up in Elvendale: up in the mountains on a grassy plain with our backs up against Shaumbra, the crimson dragon.

"You can open your eyes when you're ready."

Kong opens his eyes and gazes out on Elvendale, the forests, the fields, the river that slinks its way to the sea on the horizon which we can faintly see far out. Elvendale City is sitting on its mountain peak in the distance to the left, with a long, elevated bridge leading up to it. The city is shining white with its blue roofs, window-panes, shutters and doors as a beautiful contrast.

"Wow, from this spot Elvendale is so overwhelmingly beautiful."

"Julia had you on a flight with Loong, right?"

"Yes, it was wonderful. One feels so free and light,

and totally without fear."

"Today you'll meet the crimson dragon, Shaum-bra!"

"Oh, when will it be here?"

I feel Shaumbra move a little as she answers in a gentle, female voice.

"She is already here. You lean up against her."

Kong gets half up and turns his head. He looks a little worried.

"Oh, well. Hello, Shaumbra."

"Hello, Kong. Luzi insists on me being a female!"

"It suits your gentle nature!"

"You're always so funny, honey!"

"You're really in a good mood today, Shaumbra. Rhyming and all!"

Kong is just sitting there in awe of the red dragon with the leathery skin. Shaumbra reads my mind.

"The lady in red in all her glory!"

She starts to laugh, then I join in and then Kong. Shaumbra turns her head slightly to the side.

"You can touch me, Kong. I can bite, but I wouldn't... at least not for the moment."

Kong stands up and pats the large dragon. She is lying down, but her back is still over Kong's head so he can't see what lies behind her. She addresses him.

"You're here, Kong, so you can finish a part of your human life and move on. I know that you still must meet with Ting and the others, but that is just a detail. I could show you glimpses of one of your other lives, but I choose to tell you about it instead."

Kong sits down beside me. Shaumbra turns so they are face to face. She doesn't speak with her mouth, but they look each other in the eyes.

"In another life, you had lost your wife and kids in a fire and, for that, your wife's family punished you severely. This was the incident you reacted to when your house and store burned down. It was an automatic response you started, shutting everything else out and freezing to a standstill."

I quickly jump in.

"This is the explanation for your reactions, not a judgement in any way. You must understand that."

"Oh dear, yes, of course. It makes perfect sense. What a lot of suffering and pain for nothing."

Shaumbra uses a firm voice.

"Look me in the eyes, Kong! Don't judge the man you were. He had no guilt in this matter. It was not his reaction, but the reaction of a memory. Your soul doesn't judge you and nor must you; ever!"

We hear a female voice coming from somewhere behind Shaumbra.

"Hello there?!"

We look the way the voice comes from. I know it is Julia.

"May I join you?"

Kong is taken by surprise. Julia wears a light-blue dress of thin fabric reaching below the knees, loose hair, silver sandals and no jewels.

"Oh, Julia. Yes, yes!"

Now the last strings lose their hold on Kong, even though he does not recognize it.

"I have to ask you something, Julia!"

"Yes?"

I know that Julia knows what the question will be.

"I have to ask you about Mary Magdalene."

"Yes?"

"Is Mary Magdalene a part of you?"

"Oh, I don't have a part of Mary in my essence. It's more the other way around, but that is not relevant, ever."

I could clearly hear the full stop at the end of the sentence. It was said in a kind voice, but it was clear that this should not even cross his mind again. In a way, I understand her. It is only a distraction to him, and she is herself and nobody else. I take over to clear the energies.

"Julia, it is special to be here with you and, at the same time, knowing that your body is still just a few cells growing inside me."

"You know it's a human thing: body equals me! What you see here isn't even me, I just like to play with my life and body to come. I look forward to 'play' from your side of the veil, so to speak."

What a different and much more mature appearance than I'm used to. Very firm in a way, and with clear borders.

"I wonder if it will be difficult for me to change diapers on a baby and talk about grown-up subjects at the same time?"

"Dear Luzi, Mum, you'll find that you can't talk about grown-up stuff when you're handling a baby, and you really shouldn't. I'll remind you, be sure of that!"

Kong looks broken-hearted.

"I feel that my behaviour when Ju-long was a child ruined his childhood."

"Grandpa! This HAS been explained to you. Humans have billions of aspects from maybe a thousand lives or more. If you need to blame it on somebody, blame it on the one who actually acted at that moment. Blame it on the guy and forget all about it!"

That was down-to-earth talk: You lost a game of tick-tack-toe – get over it and move on. In the view of the Master in her great wisdom, the incident is just one out of so many.

"In the view of one incident in all your lives of so many, and the same goes for Ju-long, it had only little weight in the grand total of your wisdom. The same goes for the responsibility for a child."

Julia takes his hands and looks him in the eyes.

"Children come not FROM you, but THROUGH you, you being a man or a woman. You lent the initial genes and upbringing, but you can in no way claim the ownership of ANY souled being; their life is THEIR responsibility, don't try to take that away from them."

"I'm an old man, it might take some time to sink in."

I can feel that Julia knows exactly what to say.

"Yes, you're old, but I'm not talking about Kong. I'm talking about your wisdom. Here is a paradox because, when removing time from the equation, ALL the experiences on Earth feel to have started recently."

Kong smiles. He really loves his granddaughter. She lets go of his hands and touches his cheek. She smiles.

"Are you not supposed to be out on a fishing trip?"

"Well, yes!"

"Then you should do something about it, Grandpa. You're the fisherman!"

We are right back on the boat; we didn't even say goodbye. Well, they are with us anyway, so to say goodbye is kind of silly.

Kong looks around and I gently put a hand on his shoulder.

"Slowly, get up. Take my hand. She's really a handful, our Julia!"

"You can say that again!"

"And I thought I was tough! Ju-long will agree with that."

It seems that only a few minutes have passed and, as we walk back to the others, we see that they are just leaving the table. Kong is very joyful now.

"Let's catch some fish!"

And we do. We end up with a couple of mahi-mahi, more mackerel, and Kong got the only barracuda, a large and fierce one, but I guess they always are. We flay the fish on the way back and reach the pier in Aberdeen Harbour at precisely 4pm. As we are standing on the quay waiting for the car to pick up Kong and Mr Kwan, Kong gives me the bracelet. Ju-long and I are very impressed by the result, now that all the tiles are painted and, when Ju-long puts it on my wrist, it fits perfectly. I know that, to all of us, it has been the time we have worked together and got to know each other that has been the most important part of it; the bracelet is just the tangible symbol.

Tonight, dinner with fresh fish will be at Grandma's place, with the elders in her group and us: Mum, Dad, Anna, Ju-long and me.

After a lovely dinner, where Grandma seems happy with her new arrangement, I tell Ju-long about our meeting in Elvendale.

When we are in bed, he looks me in the eyes.

"So, our daughter is someone to be taken seriously when it's needed. Like you!"

"Yes, a tough gal, as you've learned I can be, but always with love in my heart."

"Tomorrow, Dad will meet Mum and Cheng, the last fearful step on his way back to himself."

Kong's future

On Wednesday, shortly before 3pm, Ju-long and I pick up Kong in a taxi at his home. Mr Kwan will not attend, as Kong feels he is not needed. Deep Water Bay Beach is a thin strip of about 500 yards of sand east of Aberdeen. Further to the east, Repulse Bay has a larger, sandy beach, but we are not here for the beach.

Ting and Cheng are waiting for us at the parking area. I sense into the atmosphere and it feels like a reunion; joyful, open and inviting. I am surprised, but then I remember the huge amount of clearing that had happened before this meeting. Cheng, who is a total stranger to Kong, is simply being himself as I have come to know him, smiling, joyful and open. We are all surprised when Ting gives Kong a hug.

"This is one of the ways that Luzi and her family have changed our way of living. I'm truly happy that you're with us."

As Ting lets go of Kong, I lay my right hand on his chest, the one with the Mah-jongg bracelet.

"My family has a lot on its conscience, and now you're all becoming a part of it. Anna has called us 'system-busters' lately."

With his hand, Cheng points across the road to Coco Thai, a small restaurant at the beach.

"We've reserved a table in the shade. Let's find our seats and maybe order something."

As we shuffle the chairs to sit down, Ting notices the bracelet.

"Oh, is this a new bracelet?"

"Indeed; a united team of skilled craftsmen and a woman has created this fifteen-piece artwork in the name of unity of our families. Kong, Ju-long and I, and with lovely support from Julia, the first to be born in this unity."

I take it off and hand it to Ting.

"It's beautiful. Oh, here is Loong, I suppose?"

Kong reaches over the table and points at some of the tiles.

"Yes, the white one. The red one is Shaumbra, who's quite a woman. The woman in gold and yellow is Julia as she looked the first time I met her!"

I suddenly feel the urge to find out more.

"Who are the other women, Kong?"

"Yes, you see, the pink one is Ting, the one in the blue dress is you and the one in red is your mother, Ya. Without her, things would have looked different, I guess."

Ju-long is curious.

"What made you select these colours, Dad?"

"Besides Julia, who wears the golden dress, I chose the blue from the colours of Luzi's eyes, the red for Ya, because I feel she's like that with some gold. And pink for Ting… well, because that is Ting… to me, anyway."

I am impressed.

"To me, you hit it spot on. Even my mum, whom

you have not met yet. May I challenge you about my younger sister, Anna, whom you haven't met yet either, even though we've spoken about her?"

Without any hesitation, he brings forth his answer.

"Red, like your mother. She has a certain fire, but there are no yellow flames."

Ju-long smiles.

"You truly have an intuitive insight, like any artist must have."

We have a lovely afternoon. Many subjects are touched on, of which no-one feels awkward. Ting and Cheng's home is officially open to Kong, and Cheng suggests a possible connection between Kong and my grandma artistically, and maybe her retirement home will need his skills to bring new ideas and methods into play. A great idea, which I hadn't thought of myself.

As we call Mr Kwan this evening, we tell him about the exceptional way everything unfolded at the meeting with Kong's former wife and her present husband. Ju-long asks him how he might see his father's immediate future, and I am relieved to hear his answer.

"We can't put Mr Wang in an apartment and expect that suddenly he can take care of himself, even with a pension. The mind is fragile and we shouldn't play hazardously with his health. At the same time, we must not put a lid on his creativity and openness socially."

Mr Kwan also tells us that Kong is very touched by the warmth and openness with which he has been received.

Anna, Mum, Dad, Ju-long and I are dining at a small Italian restaurant in the Aberdeen area, next to the sports ground. The food is very good and the staff kind and attentive. We are all excited by the changes in Kong's life.

Anna smiles.

"So, I'm red? Well, he's right though! When will we meet him? Does he even have his own phone?"

Ju-long explains.

"He has had no use for one until now, but he should have access to the Internet, so we can communicate with him when we're back in England."

Dad sums up the rest of our stay.

"Tomorrow, Thursday, is the last day that is totally free; on Friday we'll spread Grandpa's ashes, but it would be possible to visit Kong, and on Saturday we're leaving."

Mum wants to plan it out.

"Ju-long, could you text Mr Kwan to present our

options? It's past eight, so you probably shouldn't call him."

The next morning, as Ju-long checks his phone, there is a text message from Mr Kwan. Kong would like to meet his new family today, if possible.

"I'll call him right away and agree on a time to pick up Dad."

The phone rings and Ju-long looks a little confused for a moment, because he was about to phone out, then he answers it. It is Ting, and he turns on the speaker.

"Cheng and I have talked about whether we could all meet with Kong today or tomorrow: gathering the whole family. We have plenty of room, both indoors and in the garden, and would be happy to host this event. What do you say about that?"

Ju-long looks at me. I find it a splendid idea and I sense Julia smiling in the wings.

"Oops, someone must have slipped in an idea!"

I talk loudly to ensure Ting can hear me.

"What a great idea; Ju-long was just about to call to arrange something with Kong."

I see Julia with her head on one side and a cunning smile on her lips.

"Why not have everyone join in on a cooking experience, like your family tradition?"

I pass on the idea.

"Why not have everyone join in on a cooking experience, like it is tradition in my family?"

"Oh, yes. You told us about that. Cheng and I do this frequently. Come any time; we'll talk about the menu and do some shopping. It sounds great. Let us know when you know the time!"

"We will; bye Mum, and thanks."

Things happen fast. Ju-long and I are still sitting on the bed, looking at each other like, "What just happened?"

"You can blame it entirely on your daughter, Ju-long. She brings forth the ideas and we must work them out. You call Mr Kwan and we'll talk with the others at breakfast. I'd best text Anna so she'll be up. We'll call Grandma after breakfast; it's still early."

Things can move fast when you have someone behind the scene to push the energy into place. I choose to jump to where we all roll up in front of Cheng and Ting's house in the van at 11:11am. We are Grandma, Kong, Anna, Mum, Dad, Ju-long and me. I see a golden glow coming up from the garden behind the house, and know that Julia is making her own preparations for this meeting.

After the greetings Cheng leads us out into the garden, where we can sit around a large table loaded with all sorts of treats and drinks. In the middle there are loads of cookbooks and recipes, in case there should be any lack of imagination.

As the time comes to pick a shopping team, Anna talks Kong into being a part of it and Cheng volunteers to join them. My sister shows herself to be more intuitive than I would have given her credit for in her way of orchestrating this task. Later, she also talks with Kong about getting him a smartphone to ease the communication between England and China. They will work it out tomorrow.

We have the most wonderful day, with lovely food and drink, cooking and baking. Many subjects are discussed and many stories are being told. Grandma and Kong will work something out with their handicrafts. When we are back in the van after having said goodnight to first Kong and then Grandma, I see the clock showing 11:11pm. I have no words that can describe what I feel when I sense into what the day has brought. I sense Julia's gentle smile and a 'thumbs-up' for mission completed.

Back in our room at the hotel, I ask Ju-long to undress me since I feel so tired, even though it is in a good way. I remember that, shortly afterwards, I fall asleep, spooning with my wonderful man and full up after a lovely day.

It is Friday morning and our stay in Hong Kong is nearly at its end. This last day we will scatter Grandpa's ashes in the Gardens of Remembrance at Cape Collinson, on the other side of the island. We take the Tai Tam Road, first to the east then north over the mountain, and then again east to Cape Collinson Road. We are only my family and Ju-long.

The ashes are scattered in a peaceful atmosphere with tweeting birds, sounds of trickling water and a gentle breeze in the trees. Grandpa's soul is not present, as we have already said our goodbyes.

On our way back, we visit the Shek O Country Park, but without any long walks along the trails. Anna must get back to Kong so they can get him a smartphone.

Tomorrow we will leave Hong Kong International Airport at 8am, with one and a half hours' stop in Bangkok. Because we must get up quite early, we use this evening to say goodbye to Kong, Grandma, Ting and Cheng.

Nikola Tesla

Ju-long and I are back in our home in Brighton by the English Channel. We have started our work again and I am in London to follow up on my work at the university.

Right now, I'm taking a break to send an update to my friends in China about my pregnancy and the trip to Hong Kong: Ling in Beijing, who had helped me with the term 'Sidhe' in an attempt to distinguish them from the fairies, elves, dwarves, gnomes and other nature spirits, and Josephine in Shanghai, with a special hello to her grandma and the cat, Loong, for bringing the dragon into my gallery. After sending the last email, I remember that I have neglected my dear friend, Cassandra, here in London, and decide to call her right away. She is two months pregnant and I want to meet her to exchange experiences.

Soon after, Cassandra and I meet at *Ciao!*, each ordering a large, spicy chai latte. The weather is not particularly warm, but the sun is out and we are sitting outside in a sheltered corner.

I had planned to drop the news about Julia some way down the line in our talk, but I simply can't wait and must blurt it out right away.

"I'm going to be a mum, too... to a girl named Julia!"

"That was fast. I suppose that Ju-long is OK with it?"

"He had been giving it more thought than I, when I brought up the subject."

"How can you already know the gender?"

"I met her in a dream; in several dreams, actually. She chose the name herself. She said that it was the three first letters in her father's name and the last two in mine, Lucia."

"I really don't know what to say, but I really hope you are right about the gender. Do you feel sick or anything?"

"I don't have morning sickness at all. I actually feel more balanced in my digestive system than before I got pregnant. It is as if Julia makes sure that her body gets the best conditions to develop, and I benefit from it."

Now will be the time to decide if I should tell Cassandra what really happened in Hong Kong, or if I should give her the simple version. I sense Julia resonating "How can you be in doubt?" If I choose the simple version, I will not be honest and energetically push Cassandra out of my life in the long term because I, in a sense, will have to keep up the charade.

"Let me hear how you are doing regarding your pregnancy and Karl, and I'll tell you about Hong Kong later."

"I'm feeling remarkably well and Karl is wonderful. He really looks forward to being a father. Furthermore, we have decided to give birth in water."

"Oh, I've not thought of that. Tell me about it!"

"First of all, it's great to do exercises in water, especially when you gain more weight. I have already started swimming and will join a specific programme later."

"Strengthening your body by swimming and doing exercises in water is one thing, but to give birth is quite another."

"You can decide to only have labour in the water or choose to birth there as well. You will be using a birth pool, which is a large, circular tub. Water birth reduces stress on the mother and the baby, as the warm water is soothing and comforting. You can look it up on the Internet."

"Cassandra, what has changed since you became pregnant?"

"I do not sleep as well as I used to and my dreams are sometimes pretty strange, sometimes even scary."

I come up with a suggestion.

"You could write the dream down to bring it from the subconscious to the conscious mind; then get up and do something practical for a short while."

"Now please tell me about Hong Kong!"

I try to make it as short as possible, but it takes me another chai and my favourite bagel with bacon, egg, curry dressing and salad before I can finish.

"Even if you don't know what to think about Julia, you must accept that the experiences are real to us... well, or there is mass hysteria in both families."

"If I choose to believe it, it's not so difficult to put logic to it. If the soul is consciousness and the human gets one when it is born, this soul can exist without the human; the soul exists regardless of the human."

"Yes, and reincarnation doesn't even have to be part of it."

It has become late, and both Cassandra and I have to part for now. She must do some shopping and I have a train to catch.

Sitting in the train, I have some time to burn and I start to think of the construction called a 'human being'.

I am still wondering how it is that the mind and our thoughts have so little creative power to manifest our wishes in our day-to-day lives. It seems to me that our thoughts and emotions take up only so much of our time and are merely a distraction through our day.

Without these loops of thoughts and emotions, there would be so much time to be creative and truly LIVE. These loops really get in the way of true creativity and joy in life, and take up so much of our energy! I see that we have an energy crisis which is being mirrored out into this reality as a fuel shortage! Humans are still, for the most part, using dirty energy sources to propel their lives.

Now I decide to search the Internet with the topic, 'clean energy'. To be more imaginative, I choose to see the results in pictures and not text. The pictures that show up are mostly in blue colours; blue and green. Interesting. There are a lot of windmills and solar panels. If we should get all our energy from these two sources, the whole planet would be covered with windmills and solar panels, and I don't think it would be pretty in the long run. From solar panels, I am now led to the Tesla company's solar roof-tiles, which do not look like typical solar panels. From this experience, I search for "Nikola Tesla", and get a lot of portraits of the inventor and other related stuff. Mr Tesla is easily recognizable, and I bring up a large picture of the man. I see a subtle smile on his face, as if he is enjoying the moment. He is looking directly at me. Then I feel him; a very joyful and lovely feeling, and am quite surprised. At the same time, I sense a clarity or sharpness, and what I might explain as universal wisdom.

I decide to ask the genius about thoughts and feelings, even if it was the subject of energy that had led me to him. The response comes immediately and in a gentle 'voice'.

Nikola Tesla

"I AM, but I am not the human known as Nikola Tesla. I am the consciousness that worked WITH and through this human, and Nikola was indeed aware of my presence."

I am now presented with different subjects, as if Tesla has picked up on my previous thoughts. In the following, I place headlines to tell of the content and to keep the subjects apart. You may see that some of it is mentioned earlier, the latest by Julia.

Brain versus consciousness

The brain is the physical organ and the mind is what it does, its work. This work is producing thoughts and feelings. They are not real feelings, but emotions, artificial feelings produced via chemicals in the brain.

The brain thinks it is so smart, capable of original

246

thoughts, feelings, imagination and creativity, but it can work only with things and concepts it already knows.

The brain/mind is always looking for flaws and traps, things that do not fit into the picture, to protect itself from being tricked. The picture is generated from past experiences so it, by nature, will fight everything new. This is counterproductive to development and creativity.

The brain/mind is trying to mimic consciousness: it wants to be a creator with real feelings and NEW thoughts, but it lacks true imagination and, as I said, can only build on the past. The mind's creative expressions will only be a patchwork or collage of old pictures. There can be different collages, but only a few compared to the almost infinite possibilities of consciousness. The mind cannot start to fathom the amount of possibilities the 'divine' consciousness produced when this creation we call everything was brought into existence.

The mind's thoughts are mostly a loop or spiral between itself and emotions, as you stated earlier. An emotion leads to a judgement (good/bad) thought, and that thought starts an emotion which leads to another thought, and so goes the loop. There is very little creation here, if any.

Pure consciousness is an instant creator, and each imaginative 'thought' leads to an immediate creation. Real creation comes through your consciousness, not your human awareness. Let us use the word 'awareness' to label the mind's artificial consciousness. The mind is aware of itself, to some extent, as of the human senses. This awareness can be counted as one human sense, so the brain is a sensory organ and the human senses are just extensions of the brain's nerve structure.

Most life IS outside this loop, but the mind can't see through the illusion of the solid, structural world. It can't comprehend that the material world is made of a fragile energy structure where NOTHING is solid, or even 3-dimensional.

A free mind

I slip in two questions that just come up.

"Can the mind be free and still exist? IS the mind the persona?"

Below are Tesla's answers.

"The mind needs purpose and uses the noise and the stimuli of the world to find or create this purpose. It uses the noise to judge the world and build the persona. Without the judgement, the persona and the mind have no purpose and, without purpose, the mind would 'die'.

"You can exist as a person with your humanity, but without the persona which is the mind. You have the brain as 'control centre' for the body, and you ARE the awareness. A free mind is YOU free of the mind! Remember that I distinguish between brain and mind, as stated earlier.

"As space does not need a spaceship, and the air does not need an aeroplane, YOU do not need the mind. When the mind runs out of purpose, which it finds in the noise, it will 'die', and you will be out of your mind, like in 'without a mind'. The mind can be free, if it can set itself free and be in a state where it will accept a high degree of uncertainty due to lack of control."

Personal energy

After the most educational speech, Tesla continues with the subject of energy, and we are in more of a dialogue in this part.

"As the consciousness that you may call souls appeared in this creation, it was supported by an almost infinite amount of personal creative energy to play with. This personal energy was selected to fit each soul in its uniqueness, and could not be taken by any other soul."

"Why couldn't it be taken?"

"It was designed so it could fit only this particular soul's resonance/colours, so it could not be manipulated by others. The personal energy is a lunch pack of dormant energy that never runs out."

"Why can we share the collective energy, but not the personal energy?"

"The collective energy is an illusion. It is an illusion created by mass consciousness."

"How do we work with the dormant energy to create?"

"It is the imaginative blueprint that activates the neutral energy to shape itself to whatever it might be used for."

"So, I, the consciousness, imagine something, create a blueprint and then the energies start to do the creation part?"

"Consciousness works outside time, so you have to take time out of the equation. This means that it all happens simultaneously. You can even say, that 'the thing' is already there as a possibility, ready to come into existence in this reality as soon as you imagine it."

"My mind is still working on the time-thing and can't really grasp a reality without time."

"The mind IS a 3-dimensional device, and 3D always has the time function built-in. It will never UNDERSTAND no-time, it must be so bold that it will accept or, better, allow, that there is something that IS, without being able to comprehend the issue. As you, the human, know that there is someone who is 'smarter' than you, that you can accept. Likewise, the human must accept that there are conditions that will not fit into its view of 'things'."

From energy to solid matter

I have a recurring puzzle that I surely can get answered by Tesla.

"It is said that solid matter really isn't solid at all but, for instance, a rock seems pretty solid to me, especially when I give a large one a kick!"

"Let me give your mind something to work with. Solid matter is both a strong and a weak construction at the same time. The hard rock is but an illusion made through an agreement in the 3-dimensional makeup. It communicates how the world should perceive it, for instance: 'I am rock-solid', so you hurt your toe when you kick it hard. 99.9999 % of what seems to be matter is empty space. This should tell you that things can't really be solid and be strong. Imagine that you build a house by combining hair-thin sticks, but only at the ends, like building a three-dimensional grid. If there is one metre between the connections, the sticks have a diameter of only 1/10,000 of a metre. That house doesn't seem very strong. This means that it is the energy that gives the strength to the building and keeps it from collapsing, not the very thin sticks."

"But this is not what I experience in my life!"

"It's because it's not the truth if you look at it from a pure energy standpoint. You must see energy as communication. It communicates HOW the world should be perceived, like DNA tells the body HOW to behave."

"Oh, like program code tells me how an application works on my computer. It comes to mind that Ju-long is playing 3D-games on his computer that really look like they happen in a 3-dimensional world that one moves around inside, performing different acts."

"A very good analogy. You really can't say that the program code is solid in any way. It's just the agreement in mass consciousness that allows the experience to seem real. I highly recommend you to see everything as energy, and see the energy as communication. It will give you a good picture of what you experience in your life. This is how you, the consciousness, perceive things, and so you train to see life from your true self and not from a human standpoint."

AI vs. limitless energy

An obvious question to ask Nikola Tesla is about free energy.

"Some years ago, two guys proclaimed that they could produce energy by means of cold fusion. Unfortunately, the experiment could not be repeated. Can you comment on this?"

"The experiment worked, but they did not know all the elements of it, and so, when the experiment was repeated by themselves and other scientists, something was missing. They didn't take into account that there was a large transformer close to the lab that generated the exact frequency at the specific time."

"Oh, there must be more frequencies."

"There must be a resonating frequency for each chemical component that is involved in the process. If, for example, you want to split water into oxygen and hydrogen, you must resonate the water to the point where it agrees to split, and the two frequencies to draw out the oxygen and the hydrogen. You can compare it with two magnets, each with specific features to attract a certain type of mass."

"In the process you just mentioned, one could pour water on the car and use the components to run the engine?"

"Yes, that would be the first step. The next step is that the water itself knows what you want from it, so you don't have to put all this control onto the process. Sadly, it does not seem to happen for a long, long time in this evolution."

"I can imagine that it will take some time for the scientists to tell water what we expect of it, but there is a lot of effort in the energy research. What do you mean by 'this evolution'?"

"For some time, the two major paths in development have been energy and computer power, like in artificial intelligence, AI. There is not much doubt that the AI and improvement of the human body will sweep the energy research off the tracks, only using it for efficient power to robots and technology to improve human life. Computers are now far more efficient than the human brain, and the memory capacity and computing speed will make the AI much better than humans at, dare I say, all tasks."

"But humans do still need each other for multiplying, and it's still us who program the robots."

"When AIs become more intelligent that any human, it wouldn't take long before they saw the logic in them writing their own code. What happens after that we will not go into; and remember, this is only a possibility."

After Tesla has painted this dark picture of the future, I sit quietly for a while.

"Dear Luzi, we will end this meeting but, when you later are editing the text we have created, you will find some repetitions and it is as it should be. The mind picks up a little knowledge at a time, then it pieces together the puzzle and gets the 'aha'. The repetitions are slightly different angles that serve as different pieces, even though they are talking about the same, one thing."

I feel a great love from this consciousness that I still choose to call Nikola Tesla, and I know that it is not the last time that we will meet. His response comes before I have even started to write this paragraph!

"As you feel our connection, I do too. We share a great appreciation of the work we do together to lift the human consciousness to new heights. And, indeed, we shall meet again!"

I still have my phone in my lap when I change

focus to the interior of the train. I check the time, 6:33pm, which is just before I must get off. I gather my things and walk to the exit.

At the station I pick up my bicycle from the locked bicycle compartment and head for home. I do not always enjoy the trips to and from the station, but they always freshen me up and make me more present in my body. I feel more vigour when I come home, and motivated for the tedious tasks waiting.

Even though my conversation with Tesla was interesting, I clear my mind, only using my body's senses to take in all that is happening around me during the short ride home.

There is light in the house when I arrive. Ju-long is home and, by the smell I pick up when I walk through the garden gate, I can tell that he is preparing dinner. I could use a glass of wine. I park the bicycle in the shed and walk in.

Ju-long dries his hands on the apron and gives me a hungry kiss.

"You look adorable, dear."

"You too, in the flowery apron, just as you do when you're in the garden amongst your flowers."

"How are we?"

I know what he means.

"Julia and I are fine, thank you."

The main dish is fish and the wine is open; a strong, white wine from Australia. I walk to the fireplace and light the fire.

"I had a long conversation with Nikola Tesla on the train from London. Very interesting. I'll make some notes before dinner, if that's OK?"

"Yes, please do. I assume you'll tell me about it later."

At dinner, I tell him about Tesla and my meeting with Cassandra and her decision on birthing in water. Julia drops a single comment on that.

"It will be lovely to be birthed at home and in water."

"So that's the way it will be?"

"Yep! Don't worry. I'll be out before you know it!"

I tell it to Ju-long.

"Well, what is there to say? Then we'll have a water birth at home. That's actually a splendid idea, don't you think?"

I wonder.

"Would you say that she is already controlling her parents?"

Ju-long smiles.

"I would say that she already controls her life and that is great! In that respect, we are here to support her, especially while she is so young."

"This is a whole new way of parenting. One could call it conscious parenting. It sounds like a title."

Julia adds a comment.

"Indeed, I'll be your co-writer!"

Ju-long elaborates on the parent thing.

"So, it's not 'how it is done', but 'how it should be done'. The young mother can't ask her own mother HOW she should do a certain thing, she must ask her child!"

I have a great reservation here.

"But this can't apply to everyone. One must have the conscious connection or the parents would just listen to the human, egotistical child!"

After dinner we build a nest in front of the fire and spend the evening in each other's company.

Ju-long carries me to bed. It feels quite cold after spending hours in front of the fire and in close contact with Ju-long's naked body.

Energy and life

At some time during the night I wake up and take a short walk around in the house. I still have my talk with Tesla on my mind. Now I am standing looking out of the coloured-glass windows at the contours of the garden.

I sense the presence of Saint Germain.

"Greetings. Why have you honoured me with a visit?"

"As if I need any specific reason for a visit."

We stand side by side, looking out of the windows. There are four of them arranged in an arc in a niche built out into the garden. We just stand there for some time, sensing life outside in the garden and inside my body. After a while, Saint Germain breaks the silence.

"We could talk about energy and life, which seems obvious."

"Yes, please."

Saint Germain makes an imaginary clearing of the throat.

"Energy is NOT life. People think so and that is why they are convinced that they need energy to live, to survive. Life is not about having a lot of energy.

"Energy is communication; communication of how it is to be perceived. Like the computer game you talked about earlier. Music, light, money, everything is energy, but it is not life.

"Nothing happens to the energy until consciousness is present. When consciousness meets energy, energy starts moving and you have life.

"There is energy around you, but it's not group energy as stated earlier.

"Life force energy does not exist. Prana does not exist. There is energy everywhere and it is YOURS. It is nothing you must fight to get or fight to keep. Energy cannot be given away, but you, the consciousness, can inspire someone to activate their own.

"When consciousness, which is you, is present, energy starts to move by itself and you do not even have to do anything to make it flow. Energy is in service to you and will facilitate your creation of life through your passion for life. Energy is not life, but it supports the life experience. You are the life."

This inspires me to a question.

"What is your opinion on the Law of Attraction?"

"Thoughts and wishes may not correspond with your deepest beliefs, thus your dreams will not come true. Energy will flow where your focus goes. If your focus is about wanting a job, the energy will support you in 'wanting a job'. The experience of 'wanting a job' can only be met if you DON'T HAVE A JOB! That is the law of attraction!"

"So, I should focus on already having a job?"

"Yes, but why do you want a job in the first place? To earn money. And why do you want money? To buy stuff. Why go through these steps to 'get stuff'? It makes no sense. People should be smart enough to figure that one out."

The answer is obvious to me.

"The 'law' of mass consciousness!"

"Yes, the giant brain-washing machine, the hypnotizer."

"So, I must kid myself into thinking that I already have the stuff?"

"And how do you think that would work out?"

"NOT!"

"Exactly! It's the lack-factor that's in play here."

I, my human part, really start to get it.

"It is the feeling of lack that triggers the wish for stuff that then starts the 'I need to have the stuff'."

"A true creator already has 'the stuff' before she needs it, so there will be no lack at all. That is true creation and energy serving you. Energy serving you is not about what you BELIEVE, but what you

260

ALLOW!"

I am overwhelmed by the simplicity of the whole thing about creating and living.

"It is the I AM, the Master-self and the person who is experiencing and living life in trinity!"

Time is energy

I hope that I can sneak in one more question.

"Do we have time for another question?"

"Time is energy, so we have all the time in the world, as the saying goes."

I feel overwhelmed with… simplicity?

"Yes, time has to be energy! Energy is the building-block for everything in the universe, and time IS part of it."

"So, can I go now?"

I sense a smile from Saint Germain as he continues.

"You can just play the whole thing about energy all over again, replacing the word 'energy' with the word 'time'."

The concept of time is as misunderstood as the energy concept. Wow!

"If you need more time, you are simply playing

'the game of lack' as a time issue."

Saint Germain leaves me with a piece of practical advice.

"If you meet someone whom you feel you can assist, you could say: 'What are you doing with your life? Which of your actions steals your time or energy? Prioritize and choose what is important for you, not for anyone else. When you get your life back on track, people around you may very well benefit from it.'"

"I'm so grateful for this talk, and it's an honour for me to get these visits."

"It's always a pleasure… and the honour is mine!"

Feeling filled to the brim with wisdom, I walk back to bed.

What's to come

My pregnancy with Julia has reached week 15. We feel fine, my appetite has changed to different food and the health checks say that everything is fine.

I have been dreaming about baby animals, and Julia tells me that it originates from before the biology was human. This will prepare the female to be a nurturing parent. This proves that our biological vessel is, indeed, an old design.

Today it is the first Sunday in Advent on December 2nd. All rooms in the old house are flooded with the smell of Christmas.

Anna has started to have a young girl in relief care every other weekend. Her name is Monalisa; she is seven and has been diagnosed with mild autism. Today, Anna and Monalisa have been visiting us as part of a social training programme. The trip on the train went well, and we have been four people in the kitchen, on and off, baking cookies. The girl has handled the visit by us extremely well. First, I thought that to name a child Monalisa, which is so close to the painting, *Mona Lisa* by Leonardo Da Vinci, would not be fair on the child. Then Julia tells me that the name can be interpreted as The Desired Lilies (attractive lily flowers), and the girl has a connection to Fleur de Lis, France and Saint Germain. Anna also told me that it hadn't been a problem so far.

Our visitors have left, and Ju-long and I are alone in

the house. We have had long talks about the future in general and the future for Julia in particular. It is not because we are worried about the future, that is not the way we look at life, it is merely a curiosity in this time of great, even accelerating change on the planet.

We have been talking about the discarding of our ancestral DNA and the general strings to the ancestors. I have told Ju-long of my talks with Tesla and Saint Germain about energy, consciousness, the mind, Artificial Intelligence, matter and time. Now there is Julia, who changes her own biology and the releasing from the gravity of mass consciousness and its hypnotic overlays, or lies, if you will.

By bringing the I AM, which is the consciousness, the Master which is the wisdom, and the person, who is the experience device together, this trinity will be the optimum creator operating in its own creation. This gives us the opportunity to think from consciousness rather than just from the brain.

When allowing the wisdom of the Master into our human lives, we change our relationship with energy and time, which will bring energy and time into our life at the exact right moment, so there is no need for us to go out looking for it.

My alarm clock says 3:30am, as I wake up lying next to Ju-long. I have thoughts about the future bouncing around in my mind. The thoughts are persistent, so I take the chance to contact Saint Germain.

"Could you say more about what we may expect in the future like, say, in Julia's lifetime?"

The Count shows up before I have finished the question.

"I could hear your mind cranking away all the way to the Masters' Club, where I am spending this evening."

"Well, sorry."

"I'm just teasing you, Luzi. I can be at the Masters' Club and here by you at the same time. There is no space and there is no time, remember?"

"Yes."

Saint Germain continues.

The AI will become one thousand times more intelligent than humans and the AI brain will be one thousand times faster than a genuine human brain. That is why we need to invoke mass consciousness with 'enlightened' awareness. This is your real purpose. That is why you waited centuries to integrate the I AM, the Master and the human. Now you know why there are so many sci-fi movies about AI and the fears around it."

"What will happen when AI's intelligence exceeds the human's intelligence?"

"At that point, humanity will not be fully in control, and some mad people will probably use the AI's full potential for their own gain and their own vanity. The masses won't see it coming and, in the end, they don't care."

"Let us hope that the AI will do something about the mad people. Why won't people react against the AI's superior intelligence when it becomes the dominant 'race'?"

"They'll be too lazy, and will just keep living in the comfort that the AI delivers."

"So, the AI will live forever, even if humanity becomes extinct?"

"AI will reach its limit when there is no more data to collect. It will, in a sense, go mad and destroy itself."

"I suppose that will cause a total breakdown of how people are living, because they have become dependent on the AI."

Saint Germain brings the dark colours to the canvas.

"There might be other, not so glamorous scenarios, some that have been played out in countless movies: the total breakdown of governments, resulting in chaos and anarchy."

"The life for survival once again! Or people might turn in the opposite direction and choose a sustainable life with nature."

"You may be right, Luzi. This might turn people's focus and consciousness to nature's processes and how it works. Then the beings of consciousness who manage the Earth can truly turn their focus to other things and continue evolving. Gaia can then totally release her connection to Earth, which she has been governing for so long."

I get an idea.

"Humanity might evolve to be artificially created humans with a soul, by breaking the old, biological blueprint."

"That is surely a possibility. The body can work without a soul because everything, animate or inanimate, has an awareness of itself, but the body has the purpose of the soul by being its vessel!"

"I know we have talked about it before, but how can I fulfil my purpose?"

"You must be in the centre of your own creation to go through the immense changes that have already started. Your human part must join the I AM and the Master."

"I see. If I work using only my human awareness, it won't make much of a difference."

Allowing, Un- & AND

Saint Germain finds a new way to explain things to me.

"An average human's awareness is singular, because it has focus only on the immediate. The consciousness which you ARE experiences in a multi-faceted way. Symbolically, we could say that the human can only see one side of a non-transparent cube at a time, while consciousness can see all sides of the cube AT THE SAME TIME, as well as the edges and the corners, both inside and outside. This is the AND effect."

"I don't see how a person can ever be able to see all sides of the cube at the same time."

"We have to remember that the cube is just a symbol. It is about sensing into the life. To gain more awareness, the person must release his limitations by allowing the possibility of a much grander world than he has been led to believe."

"So, allowing is the thing to do. How?"

"There is no HOW to it. I ALLOW and no more. No thought, nothing; it will just put a limit on the allowing. The human allows the consciousness, the I AM, to unfold its full potential in the human's life."

"So, it's really not the person who creates its life; it's the consciousness. The person only puts limitations on its life!"

"Exactly! The person should get out of his own way to start the optimum flow. The only responsibility for the human in life is to allow it."

"But if you don't allow what you want in your life, how will you ever get it?"

I sense that the answer is obvious to Saint Germain.

"When you allow, you allow EVERYTHING, so how can what you want not be included?"

Well, I cannot argue against that one, and state what I make out of it.

"It is a team effort, then. The I AM manages the flow and the creation of the human life, and the person lives that life!"

I sense a great, big smile.

"Yes, the human goes from a solo performance to a team performance with the I AM."

"Life changing is inevitable then. I assume that everything in a human's life will change, but will it always be for the better, seen from a human perspective?"

"When life starts to flow, things get easier for the human, even if the changing may not be what the human expected, but the human's priority changes, so it doesn't matter. What was previously important has no longer value, focus changes and one's self-realization takes a quite different direction."

That remark makes me think.

"One will become a different person. This will influence both that person and the people around it, and may change their relationship."

"You said it before, Luzi, but I'll say it again by

placing a disclaimer right here. When you allow, things change, and humans generally fear change. If you REALLY step aside from the flow in life, EVERYTHING CHANGES! Are people ready for that?"

"You've asked that question before. I believe that if someone is not ready to allow fully, there will not be any changes in that person's life."

The answer comes promptly and firmly.

"You cannot partially ALLOW. The human can do his small allowing, but that will block all the other possibilities."

A question comes up.

"When co-acting in life with one's I AM, will it bring clarity and truth to the human?"

"True allowing opens to new and expanding awareness, which makes it natural to AND anything in life. Then use the AND to see that all is the truth and no one truth has value over others."

"What happens to the duality for the person who allows and does the AND?"

"Well, Luzi, let me tell you what you might not have realized about duality. You live in a reality of duality where there is an opposite to everything. Physical things, feelings and reactions. This is how you normally perceive duality, but that is just half of it. Everything has an un-thing. The chair has an un-chair, the feeling of shame has a feeling of un-

270

shame, and so on. This reality MUST have its opposite to be truly dual, so everything has its UN. It's the law of duality. This is important to realize."

"It kind of makes sense. Our reality of duality must have a balancing component, or an opponent; duality is not balanced by itself. How does the UN work?"

"The UN-thing exists shifted a little out of the wavelength of that which the human eye can perceive. In the human REALITY, matter is just energy so, in a sense, the solid thing is an illusion. Looking SOLID is the ILLUSION. The UN is not so locked into its shape as the solid one. It can move and change in size and shape. You may have experienced this, but you have thought that it was the solid thing that moved, or whatever."

"You said that it also works for feelings and everything else?"

Saint Germain elaborates.

"There is also an opposite to joy, its un-joy. You have the sad, but it has is opposite, the un-sad. The same is true for gravity and un-gravity, not that things disappear up in the air, but so it is."

"This could be the solution to the energy crisis, right?"

"YES! The UN part is actually "heavier", like in having more energy potential. It contains more reality. The UN holds things together; it's the base structure, so it has more 'weight' to it. It's easier to sense into the UN of a thing because there is more of it."

Saint Germain shows me the square as an example of the balanced duality.

It shows the true sensing or perception of the duality of hot/cold; cold and un-cold, hot and un-hot. This gives a more balanced perception, a more solid construction in duality. Saint Germain continues to build up the picture.

"To everything there is an AND, not just hot AND cold, un-hot AND un-cold. ANDs are ALL potentials. When you feel cold, the hot is also present, so you can sense into the hot to prevent freezing."

"In that example, I just believe that I freeze because I'm convinced that cold is all there is but, if I switch my sensing to the true, balanced duality, I'll get a different experience."

Saint Germain continues, like a salesman.

"And there's more! As you have you, you also have an un-you. You are not linear. Your soul experiences the lives at the same 'time'. All lives, past and future, so you live an AND live. The human is local and linear. When you ALLOW, you become part of this AND."

272

Saint Germain shows me a circle with some arrows in it. The arrowheads show that there is a linear progression in each local life. The AND is the circle where all lives are experienced by the I AM.

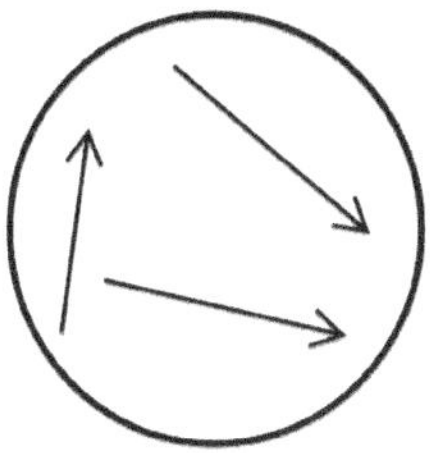

"What makes the ALLOWING and the AND work out to bring an easy life to the human?"

Saint Germain brings two new elements into the collection.

"It's based on synchronicity and the flow of New Energy. In short, New Energy is not part of duality, and therefore cannot be manipulated from a limited, dualistic point. We'll talk about New Energy later."

I agree that I feel overloaded already, but I make a note to hold Saint Germain to his word as he continues.

"Synchronicity happens with New Energy, which does not have any attributes to it, which means that it can flow into the moment without conditions. New Energy is blocked out if you pose conditions to the situation, because it MUST work WITHOUT CONDITIONS. This is also why you can't repeat a situation or outcome."

I don't know if I really like that.

"So, I have to 'start from scratch' each time?!"

But Saint Germain is excited.

"Yes! Isn't that wonderful? Then you don't have to rely on old, obsolete methods, but will use the optimum conditions every time!"

With this remark, we end our nightly dialogue and I find my way back to the bedroom.

The birth of Julia

I think it is time to bring news from Hong Kong.

We have seen Kong's drawing of Julia and Loong. It is a drawing, in black ink on heavy rice-paper, showing the dragon, Loong, to the left and Julia standing to the right with a hand on the dragon's shoulder. Kong still lives in the home getting his pension, but now he is in the workshops and on field trips as an employee. He may get an employee apartment in the complex next year.

Grandma has been quite active in the retirement home, especially with crafting things. Kong has become one of the people who often visit for teaching his skills, and he and Grandma team up, creating things together. Ting and Cheng look after Grandma and, now and then, they do things together with her and sometimes Kong is also invited.

It is Christmas and Anna, Ju-long and I are with my parents in Sevenoaks. Grandma and Kong are with Ting and Chang. This might not seem optimal, but this is how it turns out. Next Christmas, when Julia is here, Kong and Grandma will come to England. I am in my 19th week with Julia, and am mildly burdened by being pregnant. My diet has changed quite a bit and, now and then, I have an appetite like Anna's. Sometimes I feel tired because my body is working on a building project and, at the same time, regenerating itself. I visit my birth club regularly, and Ju-long and I are swimming every week. We have met with Cassandra and Karl to share experiences. Cassandra is doing fine. The cradle that Ju-long has been working on is finished. Mum has painted it in green colours with vegetation, at Julia's request. Her room is in green and blue colours. No carpets, please, again at Julia's request.

Julia is born on 6 May 2019, at 1:23pm, which is 2 April in the lunar calendar. It is a water birth in our home as we have planned. I have Ju-long, Anna, Mum and Dad around me, as well as the midwife. All the etheric realms seem to be present, including Gaia.

My body has prepared well for the event and the labour is relatively short and the pain mild, all things considered.

Julia has blonde hair and blue eyes, and weighs

6.9lbs, or 3.1kg, and measures 19 inches or 48cm. She is beautiful, and we in the family are happy to have her present in her physical body!

The End

I hope you have enjoyed the book and ask you to take a moment to make a short review on your favourite retailer website.

Thanks in advance, Eriqa Queen.

On the next page, you'll find my short comments about this book.

Author's Comments

When writing the first title in the series, *The Soul of the White Dragon*, Luzi appears as a fictional person to carry the story and present the knowledge. I could relate to the character, but there was some distance to her, like she was outside me. It is interesting to experience that, when starting to write this second title, I found the character, Luzi, was presenting herself as a sovereign person in this creation. Furthermore, I was as surprised as Luzi when she realized that she was to be a mother, and even more so when the name, Julia, came up. I didn't even know whether the child would be a boy or a girl. Julia was a special and wonderful surprise. I knew that having Luzi and Ju-long together would eventually bring forth a child, but when Julia showed up, she did not arise from a conscious idea on my part. As my work progressed, I came to realize that all the main characters are of consciousness and have their own lives that interact with me as the writer, more than growing out of an author's mind. Ju-long's father, Kong, did not show up as a consciousness until I let him open in the story. This was a special experience.

The information in this book is not meant to be adequate, but more a pointer to subjects that you can follow up on.

I have really grown close to the figures I have worked with in this book. They have all been my true and dear friends, so thanks to all of you. We, me and my friends, have been writing this book in a forum, all adding bits and pieces to the story.

- EQ

Additional stuff

There is so much material that in different ways can trigger your depths and make you remember, so this list is just some small examples.

Links

www.ancientscripts.com

Chronology of the ancient Near East: en.wikipedia.org/wiki/Chronology_of_the_ancient_Near_East

Crimson Circle: www.crimsoncircle.com

The Book of Tobit (you can find different translations on the Internet): archive.org/details/pdfy-WVasxKo7ugzzsKJL

The Gospel of Judas: www.nationalgeographic.com/lostgospel/_pdf/GospelofJudas.pdf.

The Indus Script: swarajyamag.com/culture/how-I-deciphered-the-Indus-valley-script

Songs

This song is an addition to the list of songs started in the first book in the series.

Moonlight Shadow, 1983, Mike Oldfield (Michael

Gordon Oldfield).

Books

On the Road with the Archangel, Frederick Buechner, 1997, ISBN 978-0-06-061125-1

Getting Real About Enlightenment – a modern companion to your journey of sovereign spirituality, Kim Seppälä, 2nd edition, 2018, ISBN 978-87-92980-66-3.

Films

DVD, *The Gospel of Judas*, National Geographic, 2009. The translated gospel can be found here: www.nationalgeographic.com/lostgospel/_pdf/GospelofJudas.pdf.

Sources

Here are some of my sources that you might find interesting to dive into.

Links

Links may cease to exist, but then you can search the main words and you may find an even more appropriate source of information.

www.ancientscripts.com

Dr Murray R Adamthwaite, *Gilgamesh and the biblical flood*: creation.com/gilgamesh-and-noahs-flood-part-1 and creation.com/gilgamesh-and-noahs-flood-part-2

en.wikipedia.org/wiki/Sumerian_King_List

Noah's Ark hidden in the ancient Chinese characters by Kui Shin Voo, Rich Sheeley and Larry Hovee. creation.com/images/pdfs/tj/j19_2/j19_2_96-108.pdf

Patheos, hosting the conversation on Faith. (Look under 'religion Library'). www.patheos.com

Remains from Morocco dated to 315,000 years ago push back our species' origins by 100,000 years and suggest we didn't evolve only in East Africa: www.nature.com/news/oldest-homo-sapiens-fossil-claim-rewrites-our-species-history-1.22114

Science Magazine: Were humans in the Americas 100,000 years earlier than scientists thought?: www.sciencemag.org/news/2017/04/were-humans-americas-100000-years-earlier-scientists-thought

The Guardian: Could history of humans in North America be rewritten by broken bones?: www.theguardian.com/science/2017/apr/26/could-history-of-humans-in-north-america-be-rewritten-by-broken-mastodon-bones

Books

Inanna, Queen of Heaven and Earth – Her Stories and Hymns from Sumer, Diane Wolkstein and Samuel Noah Kramer, Harper & Row, Publishers, first edition, 1983, ISBN 0-06-090854-8.

Inanna, Lady of Largest Heart – Poems of the Sumerian High Priestess Enheduanna, Betty De Shong Meador, University of Texas Press, Austin 2000, ISBN 978-0-292-75242-9.

Myths from Mesopotamia – Creation, The Flood, Gilgamesh, and Others, A new translation by Stephanie Dalley, Oxford University Press, 1989, ISBN 978-0-19-953836-2.

www.ingramcontent.com/pod-product-compliance
Lightning Source LLC
Chambersburg PA
CBHW020101310726
48970CB00002B/417